## D U P L I C A T I O N S
*and other stories*

# D U P L I C A T I O N S
## and other stories

by
Enrique Jaramillo Levi

Translated by
Leland H. Chambers

LATIN AMERICAN LITERARY REVIEW PRESS
SERIES: DISCOVERIES
PITTSBURGH, PENNSYLVANIA
1994

The Latin American Literary Review Press publishes Latin American creative writing under the series title *Discoveries*, and critical works under the series title *Explorations*.

No part of this book may be reproduced by any means, including information storage and retrieval or photocopying, except for short excerpts quoted in critical articles, without permission of the publisher.

Copyright © 1994 Latin American Literary Review Press

Library of Congress Cataloging-in-Publication Data

Jaramillo Levi, Enrique, 1944-
   [Duplicaciones. English]
   Duplications, and other stories / by Enrique Jaramillo Levi ; translated by Leland H. Chambers.
     p.   cm. -- (Series Discoveries)
   ISBN 0-935480-65-X (alk. paper) : $15.95
   I. Chambers, Leland H., 1928-    .  II. Title.  III. Series: Discoveries.
PQ7529.2.J27D8613   1994
863--dc20                                                  94-19375
                                                                         CIP

Cover photograph by Leland H. Chambers. Cover design by Lisa Pallo. Book design by Susan Wackerbarth.

The paper used in this publication meets the minimum requirements of the American National Standard for Permanence for Printed Library Materials Z39.48.1984. ∞

*Duplications and Other Stories* may be ordered directly from the publisher:

        Latin American Literary Review Press
        121 Edgewood Avenue
        Pittsburgh, PA 15218
        Tel (412) 371-9023 • Fax (412) 371-9025

Acknowledgments

This project is supported in part by grants from the National Endowment for the Arts in Washington, D.C., a federal agency, and the Commonwealth of Pennsylvania Council on the Arts.

The following stories have been previously published in translation:

"While He Lay Sleeping": *Clamor of Innocence: Stories from Central America*, Barbara Paschke and David Volpendesta (eds.), City Lights Publications: San Francisco, CA (1988).

"Duplications": *Translations* (Spring, 1989). Also in *Contemporary Short Stories from Central America*, Enrique Jaramillo Levi and Leland H. Chambers (eds.), University of Texas Press; Austin, TX, 1994.

"Suicide": *Latin American Literary Review* (July-December, 1989).

"Cycles of Surveillance": *New Letters* (Spring, 1989).

"The Face": *Crosscurrents: A Quarterly* (1989).

"The Figure": *Short Story International* (December 1989).

"The Witness": *New Orleans Review* (Winter, 1990).

"The Incident": *Sequoia* (Winter, 1990).

"Oscillations": *Sequoia* (Winter, 1990).

"The Trunk": *Crosscurrents: A Quarterly* (Fall, 1990).

"The Girl with the Motorcycle": *Latin American Literary Review* (July-December, 1990).

"The Book Without Covers": *Antioch Review* (Fall, 1991).

# CONTENTS

## Surveillances

| | |
|---|---|
| Cycles of Surveillance | 9 |
| The Figure | 11 |
| Premonition of Crying | 14 |
| The Face | 17 |
| The Smell | 19 |
| The Intention | 22 |

## Duplications

| | |
|---|---|
| The Party in the Basement | 25 |
| Suicide | 28 |
| The Husband | 30 |
| Duplications | 32 |
| When I Look at Her (My) Photograph | 35 |
| On the Afternoon of the Encounter | 38 |
| The Incident | 41 |

## Simultaneities

| | |
|---|---|
| Ocean Water | 45 |
| The Book without Covers | 46 |
| Synthesis Corrected and Augmented | 49 |
| The Offering | 56 |
| While He Lay Sleeping | 61 |
| The Reader | 65 |

## Alienations

| | |
|---|---|
| The Shoes | 75 |
| As If There Were Nothing the Matter | 77 |
| Oscillations | 82 |
| Underwood | 84 |
| The First Meeting | 86 |

## Metamorphoses

| | |
|---|---|
| Recollecting Out of Boredom | 89 |
| The Glasses | 93 |
| Lake Outing | 96 |
| Germination | 100 |
| Evasions of Death | 104 |
| Pigeons | 107 |

## Incidents

| | |
|---|---|
| The Spectacle | 111 |
| Inertia | 113 |
| The Schoolgirl | 119 |
| The Mannequins | 122 |
| The Girl with the Motorcycle | 124 |
| Witness | 128 |

## Re-Incidents

| | |
|---|---|
| Nereida | 131 |
| The Trunk | 138 |
| Her Name Is Lucía | 140 |
| Baptism in Absentia | 143 |

## New Duplications

| | |
|---|---|
| I'm in Love with You, Sylvia | 147 |
| They Don't Think I Had a Good Motive | 150 |
| The Owl Whose Wings Stopped Beating | 166 |
| While Typing | 176 |
| Shame | 181 |

... who knows if this other half of life in which we think ourselves awake is nothing but a dream which is slightly different from the first and which we awaken out of when we think ourselves asleep.

—Pascal

# *SURVEILLANCES*

## cycles of surveillance

You awaken me in the nighttime, your presence behind the door wakes me up. Other times I feel you at the head of the bed or beside it. In the street I have gotten to be afraid of your footsteps behind me, above all when they come to a stop very close by and I know you are looking over my shoulder.

I am tired of your reading books and newspapers with me, of your tasting the meals they give me. When I sing, I perceive a slight quaver that you leave there in the depth of my voice. I don't dare to speak any more because you will be dubbing in your breath over my words and I will have to recognize you in the things I say. The only thing lacking is for my innermost thoughts to also turn out to be part of that presence of yours which is growing and changing every minute, making my life impossible.

I have tried to understand the why of your watching me. Rummaging around in the past, I came to suspect that I met you in an ink blot which changed before my eyes into a butterfly that was beating its wings in a furious attempt to flee. You weren't even pretty like those that visited the garden when I was a little girl. Your wings were covered with a dull, sticky grime that got tougher and tougher the more they tried so uselessly to escape. Only your eyes were beautiful, two shining, polished balls that reflected everything around us, including my own spellbound eyes that could not stop looking at you. But I know that you were not that strange butterfly. I know because one night, after dreaming that you had managed to escape and were watching me fixedly as if wishing to pierce my dream, I found it dead upon the bed, next to my feet, eyeless. Those eyes were never able to abandon their obsessive place in my brain and soon they were recurring nightmares.

The presence that does not allow me to live is those eyes, is you, the fixation that you are transforming yourself into. You have nothing to do with the butterfly that was holding you prisoner. I no longer have to dream about you for you to pursue me. You are in each of my moves, insinuating, doubled, multiform. You are real because you have succeeded in becoming a premonition. When I find out exactly what it is that I have these forebodings about, this cruel obsession will also have fully taken shape. Then you will be able to recover your wings and fly to other worlds in order to take on from new ink blots whatever hallucinatory identity they may wish to give you. And that way you'll be able to begin your countless cycles of surveillance all over again.

Today I see you clearly in the mirror. You are my eyes, which are staring at us. We felt the beautiful strength of your penetration piercing my languid skin. We wanted to join together, even in our very blood, feigning a defense. It was too late then because you had possessed us already, I had been possessed by my very own self, under the spell of my own eyes, your eyes, our eyes, dying.

# the figure

> The disabled and the deformed upset us spiritually because they are the prefiguration of one of our possibilities.
> —Salvador Elizondo,
> *Cuadernos de Escritura*

In an almost visceral way, he was glued to the light rattle of the rain upon the glass pane, until Alma's figure took on a texture so real that he might have been able to reach out his hand and touch it, as if she were actually there instead of being a hallucination, standing in front of his wheelchair, just as on other rainy nights, watching him absentmindedly smoking his pipe.

The girl's black hair always gave off a clear fragrance of violets which he would breathe in while pretending an indifference he was a long way from feeling despite his effort not to change the direction of his gaze, which was fixed on the large raindrops sliding down the glass. By dint of concentration the peculiar sound of that interminable tropical rain managed to become so amplified in his brain that the words which Alma was articulating to entertain him a little never got to be more than a vague murmur.

And notwithstanding this attitude of his, she insisted on staying on with him until he was overcome by sleep and with his head drooped over his chest he ceased to hear the rain and her words. Immediately he would evoke the times when he would be running joyfully after her on a solitary beach until he caught up with her and would fall panting over that laughter which would burst out so infectiously. But scenes like that never lasted because soon a group of students Alma's own age would drag her from his arms and begin to kick at him on the ground while calling him an old satyr. Upon waking filled with distress, he would find her gone.

Enrique now had the impression of hearing Alma's voice again through the intermittent beating of the water against that steamy glass which would not let him see the garden she used to take care of so neatly when his illness incapacitated him. The sensation of that presence was made all the more forceful when he ceased being aware of the rain and noticed that within his head there really were words being articulated that his will was unaware of, and that just a few yards from his wheelchair a silhouette which he had formerly situated only in his imagination was beginning to materialize.

"I told you once I would always be here to care for you," he comprehended that the voice was speaking inside his brain. "It was an accident. It wasn't your fault."

When Alma was a beautiful body no part of which remained for him to explore, she had never had the obsessive reality of this figure which now permitted him to see, with such clarity that he would spend hours behind the window, the things that remained behind him in the depths of the room. Thus he was able to distinguish, directly behind the silhouette, the rocking chair where he used to rock back and forth with Alma seated complacently on his knees. And seeing her now fulfilling her promise to be with him always, he longed to make the wheels on his chair turn until he was next to her and to tell her, "Sit on my legs the way you used to do, my little girl."

He didn't do it because Alma was dead and he thought this presence seen against the window was nothing but another sign of his devastating melancholy. Then he heard again, as if this were the wished-for confirmation, a coherency of words which took on an immediate significance in his head: "I am with you, Enrique . . . You aren't imagining it."

The fragrance of violets intensified just then and Enrique was unable to resist the temptation to try to touch that figure which would not allow his eyes to rest on it. If Alma was there, if she had come back to reassure him that it wasn't his fault, it could only be because the poor thing was really unaware of the murderous force that jealousy had managed to spawn in his soul after he found himself condemned to permanent invalid status. It hadn't been enough for him then that she took care of him, that she stayed by his side on rainy nights. He knew that during the afternoons she would go out on excursions in the country with young men her own age, that her short skirts and tight blouses were not being worn for him any longer. And that was why, in a moment of anger, he had sent her rolling down the stairs, and why he was now approaching this presence that had miraculously returned in order to take care of him. He had to tell her the truth, to ask her pardon while clasping her waist. He wouldn't put up with this guilt any longer.

No matter how he steered the chair toward Alma's figure, he did not succeed in diminishing the small distance that from the first had separated them. Although he no longer was aware of perceiving any words being articulated in his brain, he continued to receive the strong odor of violets originating in that black hair which was the only concise thing in the silhouette's tireless glimmer.

He wanted to put an end to the doubt which once more was goading on his determination, and in order to prove to himself that he was not imagining things, he suddenly speeded up the movement of his hands on the wheels in an anxious effort to seize the apparition before it should fade away.

He penetrated into the darkness and there he remained, in a frenzy, turning and turning in his chair, his arms outstretched.

---

# premonition of crying

> I have sought you, I seek you, among the remains of the night in ruins.
> —Octavio Paz, *Junio*

**d**on't move. I want to remember you. At this moment you must be typing some letter that your supervisor has dictated. Or you are taking care of a client with that diligence which is all your own. Now you check over the papers he has brought, taking no notice of the gaze running over your neck and down past your breasts to come to a halt at your narrow waist. You lift your eyes and ask him with a smile if he would like to sit down, that you will call Mister Mortimer right away. You get up and walk toward the ample office. You deliberately ignore the manner in which the man follows the movement of your buttocks beneath the light skirt, the very short skirt that permits you to show off those strong elastic legs that I have always loved.

It's been so long since I've seen you. But nonetheless in my mind you go through the same routine every day. I brush my teeth, take a bath, get dressed rather late just at the moment you are receiving a long distance call for Mister Mortimer or crossing your legs at the enormous mahogany desk without paying any attention to the slight bending of your body or the lascivious shine of his blue eyes as they attempt to scale your slender thigh and get in under your skirt the moment you change position; you simply get ready to take dictation and tell him: whenever you like. I start to write while evoking the tenuous fragrance of violets given off by your recently washed skin, trying to concentrate on the metaphoric sense of the paragraph I propose to write. Every time I put down an O the exquisite roundedness of your navel is outlined clearly before my eyes, as is the diminutive periphery of the mole close to that slit which I would discover one afternoon when the monotonous sound of the rain and the willingness to be explored emanating like a mysterious breath of your longing made it no longer possible to postpone your surrender.

I don't know you now as I did in those endless kisses you used to give me, in the bittersweet taste left in my mouth by your rigid nipples, in those prolonged glances that transferred life to me and were deposited in my bones like calcium to give me strength when our parting was no longer to be deferred. I would like to think that your belly will go on being a cool pillow for my head when this separation slackens and I am able to become acquainted once more with the vast pathway of your moans. But time diminishes our promises and makes our hopes fragile.

Every night I hear crying coming from someplace and then I love you with less vanity, beyond the pleasure, the guilt. I love you, wanting to give life to the son that was unable to take shape in your womb. We would have been able to create a little corner in our clandestine relationship if it weren't for egoism; that enlarged bubble replete with the impossibilities separating your young life from my already committed one took over the unknown space where our feelings were floating. And we also denied him the opportunity to suffer—though who knows?—as well as the opportunity for many smiles as well.

I know that wherever he is he knows himself loved in the memory I keep of his mother and is attempting another approach to life. But there exists a very real distance which is insufficient merely to accept if I wish to blot it out. And my doubt, which is never completely resigned to the mere recollection alone of those hours during which we were filled with happiness, is prepared to believe that you continue to love me in spite of everything.

Nonetheless he wants to be born, I know it, and not to be put off indefinitely. And probably he instills in us new forms of inventing the future. The telepathy of expression which I pick up every day from the mirrors, the vision of your trembling flesh, every promise renewed and multiplied which I intuit through my obsessive dreams, these fill my nostalgia with dread. And in fact the premonition sometimes comes over me that this tormented emptiness of such anguished, prolonged duration will not be peopled with images of you that are still hopeful, still deliberately faithful to the memory—not unless I invent them. The deep silences that are hammering at my side show me that your voice belongs only to the far-away, everyday space in which you move.

In my dreams I begin to hear weeping anew, far off. And I wish to remain asleep, conscientiously free from waking up. I do not wish to open my eyes one day and continue to hear the awful crying of that child that would confirm your betrayal.

## the face

I saw her seated at the edge of the sidewalk. Her body, dressed in black, was a shapeless bulk bent over outward as if attempting to spread itself to the street in that mute supplication which I noticed by chance on the way to my appointment. She was hiding her face behind her left hand. After a low moan there followed a silence, and I stopped with the idea of helping her. I noticed that her other arm dangled over her thigh, a letter or maybe a handkerchief in her hand. For a long time I felt the pain in her disconsolate gesture, her weary posture so natural to those who hope for something. Some misfortune was hindering her from perceiving my presence, or perhaps she was gathering her strength to confront some piece of bad news, the arrival of someone, or the impact of some heavy grief.

She didn't feel my vacillating hand on her shoulder, nor the effort of my breathing to direct words to her. Her body was motionless in front of me; she hadn't stirred at all. Who could say what course her mind was taking?

From close up I looked at the hand hiding her features. The fingers were those of a mature woman: slender, though tightly curled over. Her black hair fell in disarray over the back of her long and very white neck, the tips blending into the mourning cloth covering her shoulders. It was a letter that she had in her hand, and I imagined a full picture of the grief she must have gone through on reading the news of someone's death. The compassion that overflowed within me was on the verge of turning into an embrace, but the fixed expression on the woman's face was stronger than my pity. It seemed impossible to break through the distance separating her mind from her body, and I began to pull back. Slowly I withdrew, leaving a portion of my distress behind next to that inert mass which was becoming blurred in the distance, as I confirmed each time I looked back.

My every encounter with the woman, who is always seated in the same posture by the sidewalk, is a repetition of what took place that first time. To get to my appointment I must unavoidably pass in front of the doorway which frames the motionless figure of the woman between two pillars. Inevitably I direct my steps toward her, place my hand on her shoulder, and make an effort to put my pity into words. I realize all over again that it will be useless, that her absence is stronger even than the presence of that hand curled up in front of her face, more real than the letter to which her other hand clings, spread over her thigh. And I depart with the same sadness, leaving still another portion of my distress beside her.

My encounters with the mourning woman are beginning to despoil me of my energy. I fear that if I continue leaving fragments of myself next to her immutable manifestation, eventually I will never keep my appointments any more. I cannot continue abandoning myself to her indifference, to her being unaware of the sorrow that identifies me with her. I know that if some day she manages to withdraw from in front of her face that contorted hand which conceals her grief, the various portions of distress I have left at her side will blend into one single, untransferrable sorrow, because at that moment they will have recognized my face.

## the smell

The cat keeps staring at him. He had noticed those narrowed eyes fixed on him ever since he opened his own eyes hours before. Or perhaps several seconds ago, he's not really certain. And it is curious that she would choose the figure in the mirror on which to set her cold, obstinate stare. Just as if she saw in the reflection of the pallid face jutting out from between the sheets a reality that her instinct would deny the true face of the man. Consequently his restless eyes see her staring at him in the wide mirror, endlessly, without blinking.

Then the man turns his head toward the mirror and his eyes encounter those of the cat there. He feels a sudden dizziness. He has to lower his sight.

When he sought again for the animal in the corner of the room from which she was observing him, he no longer saw her. But when he looked at himself in the mirror, instead of encountering his own eyes, relieved of the previous tension, he found the eyes of the cat imprisoned under his own intense, heavy eyebrows.

And they continued to observe him. Yes, observing him and lying in wait, because that's what they used to do, and they're doing it now, damn it; they're stalking me, guarding over me, condemning me. What the hell do you care if I've killed her? Of course, I know; you went to lick her face because she was your protector, the one who fed you. But she was also my wife. And the only thing she was ever able to do for me was give me those loathsome medicines. She never had a kind word for this poor devil, except in front of visitors, of course. And then she began to bring this guy in. Without the slightest explanation. She liked him, and that was it. Night after night from this very bed I had to endure the scenes they put on without the slightest modesty in front of me, on purpose, mocking me because my illness. That was why I did it, kitty, that was why. And now, in revenge you've gone into hiding and left me your eyes on my face. You're afraid that if I could move I would do to you what I had to do to your mistress, right? But you're forgetting that it wasn't necessary for me to get up to do that.

The man stopped speaking. Making a prodigious effort he raised his head a little. Then he concentrated all his attention on the haggard image reflected in the mirror. After a few minutes, the cat's eyes formed part of the animal they belonged to. The man smiled, relieved to see that her face had been exchanged for his. He concentrated once more.

The cat watching him from the mirror didn't see that the figure of the invalid, creating its own space there, had gradually managed to place itself behind her. Neither did she know that his hands were on the verge of going around her neck. She merely heard a death rattle in the room.

The man has turned his head gradually. The body of the cat is twisting and turning in the corner.

Patiently he waits for the final convulsion. A little further back he manages to glimpse a contorted hand and recalls with satisfaction the empurpled face of his wife, the impossibility of her scream.

He closes his eyes. He knows the nightmares will not be repeated any more. The relaxing is complete. Hours have gone by, perhaps even days. Suddenly he awakens startled. The smell that fills the enclosed room, now without ventilation, strikes his nose fiercely. At first he does not understand, but then he remembers. He tries to concentrate in order to create a superior smell, one that is appropriately pleasant. Something goes wrong. The stench itself is distracting him. Why hadn't he waited until she had opened the windows as she did early every day!

In the silence of that stillness, only his nostrils are moving. Their rhythm is very slow after the initial choking sensation, but now his mind is participating no longer.

# the intention

She will never understand why there is such sadness in my kisses. In her look I will see suspicion; doubt will put a desiccated trembling into her fingers that I will feel when she tries to caress me. I won't be able to bear the gaze that seeks to find out what is going on with me, and I will have to plead a logical weariness after so much extra work at the office. When she falls asleep weeping at my back, our separation will have become more complete.

All the while the images of my dream will gradually take on the contours evoked during the long trip home. In the distance the other's lips will be calling for me until the moment her figure appears, wrapped in the mists. I will narrow down the space separating us, and almost immediately I will have felt the real warmth of a mouth eager to close over my own.

I will respond to her kisses, and my body will not hesitate for long to press itself against the encircling warmth without being concerned that I have not opened my eyes to appreciate the vehemence of her gestures. Shortly afterward, my companion will be the one who, only half satisfied, will detach herself from my embrace, although my whole intention remains wound into the imagined flesh of a Graciela who will have gradually moved away until she once more becomes a remote point that will be dissolved without delay.

The dawn will come, and I will not know how to separate from my dream the memories of idyllic hours lived the previous day. But on encountering those eyes observing me from that sleepless face, the evidence that I am no longer sole owner of the secret will be as strong as the hatred that emanates intensely from my partner, reaches my throat, encircles it, and squeezes . . .

# *DUPLICATIONS*

## the party in the basement

I don't even recall who invited me, but Iowa City is a small town and it wasn't difficult for me to find the place. It was in a basement you got to by going down some narrow and badly lit steps where couples, seated or afoot, blocked your way with their bodies clasped together. The clamorous music and the psychedelic lights that burst out from below and reached the street were attracting a greater number of onlookers every moment. Some of them, especially those who were not so young, went on their way after a while, once they had satisfied their desire for novelty amid the blinking of the lights.

With great effort I managed to break through the arms which the enlaced couples were so lavish with and, inserting myself in among those bodies that took up the whole length of the stairway, I found myself suddenly in the midst of a small room. At one side a dozen couples were dancing amid the shadows. On the other side a rock group comprising several long-haired figures were swaying their pelvises about, their bodies following the frantic rhythms of their instruments. Behind them lights in a vertical tier of all colors were violently flinging their intermittent spasms over me.

For a moment I remained standing there, feeling that the lights were cutting me into long, warm striations from head to toe which inexplicably were lacerating my skin like so many handsaws. The couples formed a circle around me then, including those who had been on the stairs, because when I turned around in confusion, feeling a pleasant sort of pain in my torn flesh, I saw that the way out was now clear. I could not, did not want to run.

The music became more intense and I felt that it was dividing me, that each vertical stratum of my body was taking on its own independence but that I was present in each new part being split off from my principal being.

The center of the compact wheel that those present formed now was gradually being populated by replicas of myself that were beginning in their turn to make up another smaller circle. I continued to stand in front of the lights which went on sectioning me and hurting me and thrilling me to the point of paralysis.

I shut my eyes the better to be able to resist such pleasurable pain, assuming that everything was no more than a dream and that consequently I had no reason for hurrying to wake up. When I opened them again, the piece the long-haired musicians were playing had become slow and the couples were dancing very close together. Now I saw no more blinking lights, just a warmly inviting semi-darkness in the basement.

The man watching us from the center of the room where I had been a few seconds before had the most acute incredulity stamped upon his face, one which was totally unfamiliar to me. I understood his astonishment only when I managed to relocate myself slightly. And my surprise must not have been any less intense than his at that moment for I realized that the girls at the party were all dancing with me as if glued. I felt them in many different ways next to the many identical bodies that had been engendered from that other one which a little while before had been alone. I understood all of a sudden that the rest of the men who had been dancing when I arrived had been assembled together into the body of the one who was now flinging those hate-filled glances at the multiple forms of my being.

After having moved the girls to one side, we turned toward the intruder and, in obedience to one single idea, we threw him out of the party without saying a word.

# suicide

> Several mouthfuls make a life and one alone makes death.
> —Miguel Hernández

It wasn't something he should start thinking about now. He had to do it and that was it. No time to lose. She might arrive at any moment, and then he would not find the strength.

He looked at himself again in the mirror. He raised the gun to his right temple.

Someone was knocking on the door. He tried to pull the trigger. They kept on knocking. His finger as if frozen. They would knock it down. He couldn't. He lowered the pistol.

The roar of the explosion made him jump. In distress his eyes followed the trajectory of his dangling arm. There below, too far away, in a world defeated by inertia, was his hand, closed around the gun.

Astonished, he sought himself in the mirror. Before him, his thin figure was falling to the floor at that moment, eyes out of focus, head shattered. A sharp chill lacerated his surprised flesh, penetrating his bones.

At his back he heard the door yielding. He recognized the screams. He twisted around to make sure it was she they were coming from. Behind the bleached picture of his wife, two policemen were watching him, perplexed.

He wanted to explain to them. He was out of danger, there had been only a momentary weakness. He would never frighten her again this way. The vision in the mirror was just an optical phenomenon, a collective hallucination. Things happen like that sometimes. Touch me, he said. I'm all right. But he had the feeling that his words had remained imprisoned behind his desire to utter them.

He kept wanting to shout out to them that he didn't understand, either, that it really wasn't important. The essential thing is that I'm alive. This other situation is only a depressing warning about what could have happened if you hadn't gotten here in time. I love you, Andrea. You must pardon me. We still have time. Give me another chance. Come on, let me hug you. But the woman's screams were striking him on his open mouth now as her despair filled the room. She had stayed back a little, hands contorted in front of her face. The policemen were bending over his body.

He saw her immobility break down suddenly and she ran crazily to thrust herself into that natural background which had been the wide mirror. There she embraced the head that was loosing blood onto the floor, gushing. The policemen got up respectfully.

He discovered then that the familiar furniture was no longer around him, that the walls where one night they had hung the best of both their paintings existed in their usual place only in the background, where he had thought the mirror was. He looked at the hand which still retained the metallic sensation of the gun. He knew immediately he would have to look for it logically behind him, a few yards from the corpse.

He still tried rationally to understand the process that could make sense of the facts for him. Andrea's convulsively heaving shoulders let him know it would be useless. Between his uncertainty and her sobbing, an insurmountable sensation of finality was gradually settling over him. He would be able to resign himself to it. He felt sorry for her.

# the husband

She returned at last, after a lengthy absence. Nothing seemed to have changed in the city. But on the street that day I saw her on a man's arm. It was raining. She wore her hair longer than ever, down to her hips, soaked. His face I couldn't see because she hid it from view.

I discovered they were married because a friend who was accompanying me confessed as much when he noticed that I was getting ready to go meet her. They walked by without seeing me. The rain did not seem to bother them.

A new impulse forced me to go after them. I hastened my step. Soon I ceased being aware of the continual bursts of water that were falling more furiously now.

I had almost caught up with them already when he stopped a taxi. I ran. Sandra got in first. I was able to grab him by his jacket. He had hardly felt himself jostled when he turned around and without a second thought embedded his enormous fist in the middle of my face.

*the husband*

The taxi drew speedily away.

I doubt very much whether she realized what had happened. She was too absorbed in her newfound happiness. But I, it was as if I were lightning-struck, not so much by the blow, but out of bewilderment upon finding out who the man was that had stolen her from me.

Since then, I destroy whatever mirror crosses my path, unable to put up with looking at his face every time I see myself in the reflection. Though I must confess that I do not hate myself any the less on that account.

# duplications

It's not the first time the man passes in front of her. In actuality she has seen him at least three times, hovering around, since parking the Mustang close to the gray van she has been ordered to keep watch on. After following Li Peng all morning, who very strangely looks very much like the man who has just gotten to the corner, who is lingering there looking at her, and who now is beginning to walk toward her again, the woman seated in the Mustang is waiting for him to emerge from the Embassy. It's been more than twenty minutes since she saw him go in through the main door. The guard must have recognized him immediately, because he at once made a gesture with his head and stepped to one side. Li Peng did not look behind him as she had expected. If he had any suspicion perhaps that they were following him, he gave no sign of it.

When the man who has been looking at her gets close to the Mustang, he bends his head down to speak to her, something that surprises her greatly. It has been a sudden movement, and the woman doesn't succeed in getting her hand into her purse where she keeps her pistol. Both look silently at each other. Though still incredulous, she is able to confirm then that she is dealing with the real Li Peng, although this cannot be, since the latter has still not come out of the Embassy. And nevertheless it is he. At least, their features are markedly similar, the same baldness, an identical nervous tic in the left eye, same skin with signs of some long-ago pock- marks. And he keeps looking at her fixedly, with a seriousness that recalls the thoroughness with which she had days ago studied the enlarged photograph of the man whom she would have to follow around everywhere until further orders. But no, it can't be. She recalls perfectly that it was the very moment when Li Peng entered the Embassy that she had noticed this other man for the first time (the one who is now asking her respectfully, "Aren't you Sra. Torres, of F.I.B.R.A.?") who has been watching her insistently from the corner and who looks so much like the other one.

"I believe you're making a mistake, sir. I'm Señorita Corrales, a schoolteacher. I don't know the person you mention."

"But you are identical to the woman who spent the entire morning following the man who went into the Embassy a little while ago."

"I don't know what you're talking about, and I repeat that I don't know any Sra. Torres."

She doesn't understand how this man can know that she has been following Li Peng and yet be confused about her name. She has an urge to confess to him that, yes, she has spent the morning tailing the other man, although she is not Sra. Torres, and also that she finds an unusual likeness between Li Peng and him. But the hand of her interlocutor has already thrust itself in through the car window and is opening the purse which is on her lap. He is pointing her own pistol at her now, and with a gesture he motions for her to slide over to one side. The man opens the car door then and seats himself beside her.

They remain in silence for some minutes. Señorita Corrales begins to think that this man in reality has to be the very Li Peng whom she has been following. Perhaps she only got mixed up on seeing the other person enter the building. Her angle of vision at that moment didn't permit her to be absolutely certain. Perhaps her eyes had wandered away from the true Li Peng for the fraction of a second it took for the boy on the bicycle to go past. Yes, now she recalled that detail. And immediately she must have set her eyes upon that someone dressed in similar fashion who was approaching the guard. Which brings her to realize that she has been discovered.

She tells herself she is lost, but at that moment both see Li Peng emerge from the Embassy. He walks right in front of the Mustang and when he fixes his harsh gaze upon her eyes which are watching him perplexedly, the woman confirms that it is simply a matter of his having a face identical to that of the man who is continuing to point the pistol at her and who now is smiling for the first time.

"He's identical to you!" she exclaims, aroused, unable to hold herself back.

"It is I, my dear Sra. Torres," he says, preserving the severity of his smile.

When the shot comes, the woman realizes that the pistol still has the silencer on it that she herself had put on this morning, and she thinks that in some way she must really be Sra. Torres, so that the true Señorita Corrales would logically be that woman exactly like her who is now getting out of the other Mustang parked on the other side of the gray van, the one who is hurrying her step so as not to lose sight of that other Li Peng now going around the corner, giving up his gray van, knowing himself followed and being the owner of a face that is the faithful copy of the one owned by the man who was seated there when he shot her but isn't any longer as she falls into the space that he had occupied.

# when I look at her (my) photograph

*For Moravia Ochoa López,
a Panamanian poet*

Everyone tells me that my mother has beautiful eyes and that, if the photograph is not lying, her skin used to possess the dark exquisiteness that made Moorish women famous. Her hands were lovely too, but those only I remember. I decided to protect her face from the dust that comes in during the afternoons and I bought a gilt frame for it with glass and all. Now it's just a matter of running over it with a piece of cloth every morning, and it recovers its usual lustre at once.

The strange thing is that the day this picture was taken it was thought (at least I thought so) that it would show her full length when it was developed. I remember that she held a bunch of roses in her hands. Ramón had sent them a few hours before as herald to his arrival. Five days went by and still we were waiting for him.

And he never arrived. I was driven to distraction (we all were), unable to think in a coherent way. Mama kept some of the petals between the pages of her favorite book (my favorite): *María*.

If I talk these days with my friends about the emotions that came out of those readings years ago, they smile sympathetically, holding back their reproaches out of respect for my age. I cannot understand why modern life rejects as emotional weakness the public display that a sensitive writer re-created in an era as real as ours was. Nowadays they would have said my mother was affected (they would have said that about us). But her eyes and the slenderness of her hands (of mine in those days) continue to impress social callers. And they would all praise the exotic nobility of a complexion that seemed more appropriate to the Arab lands or perhaps to the India that we all used to dream of, so mysterious and far away.

I light the fireplace on rainy afternoons (humidity never did us any good) and her features (no longer mine) take on such an unavoidable life that at times I think the happiness she was feeling when this photograph, which she intended to give to Ramón, was taken (but we went on waiting for him; sometimes I think I am waiting still) will break through the glass which protects it from the dust (oh, if I could only protect this face too, not from time—there is no remedy for that any more—but from the allergies and the sneezing that Mama doesn't feel behind the glass) and it will come to be united with these wrinkles of mine just as in those really ingenious superimpositions they make nowadays in the movies. Then her skin (formerly my skin) on mine would in some way enact a miracle. We would live as if it were a single memory the flatteries that men would offer me on the street (that they offered her, that social callers still offer her when contemplating her picture admiringly above the fireplace). She would feel herself attractive again, with her deep black hair falling on my breasts (which no longer would have any reason to be ashamed of being so flaccid, of almost not being there at all), and covering them. And the melancholy in my eyes would light up with the enthusiastic lustre of hers (of mine when I was awaiting Ramón's arrival and had my picture taken in order to give it to him). It would be like rereading *María* in another form and weeping futilely upon comprehending that we had been left *when I look at her (my) photograph*

without Ramón, that we had lost him forever, and seeing the years go by and feeling their transformations and never knowing why he never got here and nonetheless waiting for him even today—a little old woman of my age. Because I still cannot believe (as they informed us two months later) that my beloved died of that consumption which we only used to read about in the novels of that era, that death so in vogue among the heroes.

# on the afternoon of the encounter

> Today is yesterday, is always, is untimely.
> —Octavio Paz, *El ausente*

It was in December. I did not know what form her surprise would take when she saw me standing there, in the middle of the patio, coming out of the school. I had been waiting for her impatiently for a some time.

Her letters used to come every week, lengthy and filled with longing. I read them over and over again, searching between the lines for the agonies that had spawned every phrase, grateful for her words of encouragement, her tenderness. But after a few months the tone and the length of their paragraphs began to change. Anayansi's melancholy was cooling off. And one day her letters stopped coming.

I wrote at once to all our acquaintances, to those who knew of our relationship and to others as well, friends who never suspected that the respectable Professor Valverde was sleeping with one of his students. I begged them to look her up, to ask her for some explanation. I even asked a colleague of mine, a middle-aged man whom she revered like a father, to let her know of the desperation her silence had wrought in me. Nearly every one of those who knew about my love for Anayansi brought the same answer back: "The fact is, she is so busy." Each in his own way: "You know of course she is graduating this year, and besides going to school in the afternoons, she is doing her training in the mornings, at a private firm." My friend Professor Carrillo added another detail: "In the evenings she is rehearsing for a play at the school. The poor girl is overworked. But she assures me she loves you still and that you've nothing to be concerned about. She says she'll write you as soon as she can." The others, those who had not known anything, felt embarrassed and naturally avoided the issue in their letters. In any case, Anayansi never wrote again in my five remaining months abroad.

And so that afternoon, a little after getting back to Panama, I was now waiting for her at the school with such longing that it prevented me from fixing well on the faces of the students and teachers passing at my side. She was taking a long time to come out. Unable to contain the nervousness which had me walking back and forth from one side of the patio to the other for more than an hour, I asked a student whose face was vaguely familiar to me if Anayansi Sarmiento had left already.

"But, Professor, Anayansi has been in your classroom for a long time now!" the girl responded upon seeing me, putting on an astonished air.

It gave me a great deal of pleasure that she should have recognized me after my year of absence, and especially that she would refer to that ample classroom full of little windows where I had taught for so long as if it were still mine. I thanked her and went on waiting.

Half an hour later, exasperated and on the verge now of going across the patio, mounting the stairs, and surprising her right in the classroom, without a care for who might be there or what they would think when they saw me embracing her crazy with joy, I saw her come down the stairs speaking vivaciously with a tall, rather young man, blond, wearing a gray coat and black pants, carrying a dark briefcase under his arm. I thought there was no question but that he had to be one of the new teachers the school must have hired when I and other colleagues took leaves to pursue postgraduate studies abroad.

Making an unusual effort to calm the emotion already growing in me, just as when I was fifteen and, after innumerable delays, was steadying myself to ask the first girl I was ever in love with to be my sweetheart, I approached the couple.

"Hello, Anayansi," I said when just a few steps from them.

Both looked at me. They kept on looking at me, interminably. At first I only had eyes for her, more beautiful than ever with her long hair, so very long, and black like her astonished eyes.

Upon fixing my gaze on him, however, I saw myself looking at me, puzzled.

Then Anayansi collapsed without a word.

I felt all of a sudden that my impulses were shifting, that inexplicably they were entering into that other body identical to mine which was already leaning over my beloved, which was slapping her lightly on her pale cheeks, taking no notice of the inertia that had seized my very being, turning it fragile until transparency.

# the incident

*For Jaime García Saucedo,*
*a Panamanian poet*

The glassy eyes in that livid face drew forth a pessimistic expression from my friend. I agreed that he would die before the ambulance arrived.

We had been walking along Alvaro Obregón Avenue anxious to find an inexpensive place to eat as soon as possible. On a corner we ran across a group of curious bystanders who were circled around someone. We went closer. At that moment two men were bending down over a bundle flung upon the ground. When one of them arose to ask the others to call an ambulance, we managed to see that blood was slowly welling up out of a breast which had been stabbed, soaking the shirt.

I recalled that incident today. What brought it to mind was the unexpected sight of a surprisingly blue sky with scattered white clouds, which made me forget that I was in Mexico City. I was hearing voices from all sides, I sensed shadows in movement, for they were drawing near.

Time went by and the only ones that arrived were more of the curious. It was quite evident that the man who remained close to the wounded man was unaware of any notion of first aid, and every once in a while he begged us to get further back, to let the air circulate. No one seemed to know exactly what had happened. A street fight, some thought. That guy that's with him is his brother, said another. Smells of alcohol, I remarked to Jaime. How terrible to see life slipping away and not know how to help him, exclaimed the latter.

There comes the ambulance, a woman shouted. I was retreating all the time, I am retreating, I'll stop being stretched out on the hard, warm cement before the sky falls down on me. Someone had wanted to rob me coming out of the movie, I speculated indifferently. Don't move him that way, they must have said, referring to the man with the stab wounds. Then he blinked twice with inexpressive sluggishness a little before they laid him on the stretcher. But the one who had seized me beneath the shoulders let me go abruptly, clumsily, which made me think that perhaps they were talking about me after all.

The ambulance was ready to leave when several patrolmen turned up, notebooks in hand. Their questions, addressed to everyone including the alleged brother of the victim, delayed its departure for several minutes. To think that things like this happen every day, Jaime remarked. And others worse, I added, everywhere, with or without premeditation. We began to walk. It seemed the wrong time to mention the sharp fatigue that had begun to rage within me. In the distance, the siren was beginning to blend with the sounds of the city. I sought for some little restaurant with my eyes. My friend, still a little pale, gave the impression of being submerged in a deep meditation.

He's losing blood, a voice with a twang whispered close to my ear. Heads like those of waiting vultures have hidden the sky from me. This card says he's from Panama. If I could only smell the ocean. I never saw you dance the tamborito, Nereida. Well, I could have sworn he was a gringo, you know? That poor guy left a sticky puddle on the sidewalk, did you notice? Yes, Jaime, but your food is getting cold. Let the stretcher-bearers through. The color of the sand could not be distinguished the night we took a drive out to Fort Amador and that gringo radio-patrolman suddenly came out of the darkness. This boy's not going to get to the hospital alive. You're lying, I am going to get there, I am, just give me back the clouds! Look out there, move aside please. Why the hell are they screaming so much? Before, we only used to hear the waves breaking out there, way out there, way . . .

Now I see them, thanks, they made us identify ourselves, how blue the sky is again, and in Mexico City it must be a mistake! like the afternoon when that man couldn't see any more, Jaime, when he was taken away, yes, the clouds, Nereida. I penetrate into a dark silence and the disinfectants are overwhelming me and a child is crying some place that is no longer your womb and how strange not to hear the siren any more. I am still capable of longing for my friend to confirm for me that we are still on the corner of Obregón watching an ambulance move away. And this white space that is absorbing me, where is it, and why doesn't it hurt?

# SIMULTANEITIES

---

## ocean water

The dream keeps taking more and more hold on him. After a little while he is walking along a familiar beach with very white sand. The waves lick at his feet. Then they come up to his knees. When I feel them going around my waist I have the impression of being encircled by the coolness of my sweetheart's arms. I want to preserve this illusion and so I give myself over to the soft calm fostered by my closed eyes. Suddenly he is suffocating. We get our eyes open expecting to awake out of the nightmare. But the water is already violently coming into his lungs, and then I know nothing more.

# the book without covers

*For Miguel Angel Flores,
a young Mexican poet*

I had just sold that book I found discarded among the ruins. Actually, only the covers are burned off. Every page still had the words more or less intact.

The old man in the shop on the corner bought it from me; he has all kinds of things there, dismembered and repulsive. I explained to him that Gustavo, a friend at the university, had assured me this was a strange novel, full of ambiguous scenes that allowed for a great number of interpretations. Gustavo said its ideas had to do with problems of witchcraft and since they are so well written they do really keep your attention alive. "Haven't you read it?" the old man wanted to know. "Oh, no," I said. "I am majoring in math and those things don't interest me at all." The old skinflint offered me eighty centavos for it, which I had no recourse but to accept.

## the book without covers

I should say, though later on Gustavo would refuse to accept this, that I was forced to notice that a kind of deep fascination had been coming over him as he went through the pages. I didn't want to interrupt him and decided to wait to read it myself until after he was finished. Actually, something like a fear of reading any further got into him, and he even told me the darn thing wasn't any good and I'd better just throw it out. But he refused to go into any detail; the only thing he remarked on was what I later on told the old man about the alleged witchcraft which, according to Gustavo, was the product of a morbid, deluded mind. However, I was too lazy to start reading it; the only thing I recall about it then is having noticed that the book lacked any indication of when and where it was printed, or who its author was.

The curious thing is that it wasn't burned up in the fire, as happened with all the other books in the library. Apparently they still haven't been able to determine the reason for the catastrophe. When I arrived, the rubble was still smouldering, but the body of the poor devil who took care of the place at night had already been carried away. Someone remarked to me not long back that they had found the fellow in a seated position, as if he had been relaxing. This is the first time that anything unusual has ever happened in this boring town.

They had scarcely let me know me that the shop on the corner was in flames when I had a strange foreboding. Just as happened months before, the only thing able to be salvaged was that darned book. They found the old man in the rear, stretched out on what remained of a cot, charred to a cinder. They assume that it was due to an accident although so far they haven't determined the exact cause.

The firemen were still trying to put out the fire when I got there. One of them leafed through the book while the others were arranging the hoses back on the fire truck. I assumed he was the fire chief and offered to buy the book from him. "Take it," he said with a weary face. "You can have it, I don't understand a thing." It was then that I felt a great need to become familiar with its mysterious content. My hands were trembling and in spite of all I could do it was impossible for me to keep my attention on that devastated place where not a single other curious onlooker had come. I did notice that the book, though a bit more scorched than the first time, continued to be perfectly legible.

You who are taking a brief, curious look at these timeless

confessions—I am reading now in the solitude of my own room—which you will soon take for a gratuitously imaginative creation, you must get accustomed to the fact (since it is not simply an esoteric idea, as is usually thought) that everything that is going on here has already happened, it continues happening, and inevitably it will be re-lived again in every experience that favors a re-reading. Each page is a small variation of the same phenomenon, just as you in some way have always been an alternative of some other person. This tardy discovery of the multiplicity of lives enclosed within your existence never ceases to be normal, nor that of the knowledge you are now acquiring about the simultaneity of moments one lives without knowing it. You are the character who will not long delay being touched by his exploits, just the same as he participates in every one of your acts. You will be able to recognize yourself when you meet yourself, when another reality imposes itself upon you and confronts you with what has always been going on.

Afterwards the reader will be made to feel (at least it made me think so of myself right away) that it is he himself who is living every obscure and apparently inevitable anecdote, until other individuals surface who in different circumstances continue being the one who is reading, as if everything were happening outside the text. And thus, interminably, many lives that coexist are lived without ceasing to be as independent among themselves as they are in this life in which I am still reading and in another life wherein someone (I'm not sure if it is you, he, or I) reads that the fire is all around the one reading the sentence which it is already becoming impossible to get out of, since the flames are devouring the scream you will probably have to utter when you feel my flesh roasting which you know is yours and about which, despite the fact that no one is reading any more because all the moments have been fused together, the most likely thing is that it is someone else's even though it is in us where the pain continues to be felt.

# synthesis corrected and augmented

Look, why should I kid around with a lot of quibbling, yes, I did it, or rather, I was the one it happened to. There's no reason to hide it forever. I assume that strange things happen to everyone. Though I really don't know; the truth is that sometimes I think this whole thing could only be some sort of conspiracy someone cleverly worked up just to get me involved. And I want it known that I'm not complaining; on the contrary, even though the ending did turn out to be a little embarrassing. I'm going to tell you about it because I can't stand this bewilderment by myself any longer. Yes, bewilderment: the constant sensation of living events over again and of this not being a simple remembrance of something that happened a long time ago, because suddenly it's happening all over again, at the very moment that I remember it, as for example, right now. All right then, I am walking with a friend, just as we are actually doing now, conversing then as now, side by side underneath this umbrella, without ceasing to watch the girls coming out of the lecture halls, and we are just casually going along trying to cover the ample distance that separates us from the bus stop, what a coincidence, I hadn't realized it yet, while the rain keeps coming down in torrents just like it's doing now and getting everything wet (and getting us wet too) despite the umbrella that was just like this one, yes, I even think it is the same one. We can't run because that would make it worse; there are puddles everywhere, and they say that when you run you only succeed in getting wetter, something which I have never understood very well, since you get where you're going more quickly and so you shouldn't get as wet as you do when you go slower. Well, I was saying that I was walking along with this friend, and that the girls were getting out of class in the buildings alongside of us, most of them really built (and I don't mean the buildings!), like those girls right there, see, they're starting to come out right now, it must be two o'clock already, we might connect with one of them on the bus, though we may not always have the good luck to find girls as free and open as the one with the little dog that we met that day. Ah no, well you're right of course, I hadn't told you about that yet, it happened with my other friend, the one who was with me the time I'm telling you about. The thing was, the girl caught up with us a little before we got to the bus stop. It seems she had taken her dog to class for some reason, I don't know why, she didn't have anyone to leave it with, I guess. Well, suddenly she comes up to us and says, "Don't be mean, let me put Salvador under your umbrella or he'll get a chill, you know he had a fever yesterday, the poor thing." It's funny, but that animal, a tiny Chihuahua, was encased in a red wool sweater that had evidently been knitted especially for him. He looked at us with bulging eyes that seemed to give special meaning to his owner's request, yes, you are absolutely right, just the way this Chihuahua is looking at us; where the heck could it have come from? Ah, of course, excuse me, gorgeous, I didn't hear you clearly but I can imagine what you were just saying, we understand your concern, this whole thing is a little unusual, but of course, why not? Give me your dog and get yourself under here as well, though you'll have to walk a little in front so we can all fit. Well, yes, I mean that your being here with the dog at this precise moment is a bit strange, just to call it something, but I don't think I know just now how to explain what I'm talking about because it would be a long story, perhaps just like the one I was telling my friend here, and I don't know if it makes sense, the coincidence is so strange. You haven't told us what your name is. Roxanna! oh yes, a lovely name, and besides that was to be expected, don't you think, Sergio? Look, this is my friend Sergio, my name is—but you must know it already, right?—Raymundo Quintana, and I must confess that not only your name but this whole affair is turning out to be unbelievable to me. Yes, really impossible; things can't repeat themselves this way, it's not normal. You really don't know me, Roxanna? You haven't lived this before? Well, everything except my uncertainty and the questions that I'm asking in order to understand it. No? Well, I have, I can assure you. What's more, I can tell you what is going to happen to us from now on. Do you want to know? Look, we are going to get on that bus there, because you're going to take the Bellas Artes bus just like we are, right? See? Well, the thing is that we'll just go along talking all the way, and Sergio and I will suit you to a T, so much so that you will invite us to your apartment on the pretext that you feel obligated to wash my pants since your little dog—what's his name? Wait, I'll tell you: Salvador, isn't that it?—I was telling you that he'll have shit right on my pantlegs. You don't believe me? All right, if you dare, let's do the experiment. Let's get on the bus, and you give me the dog, I mean Salvador, you really love him, don't you? Who wouldn't like to be as frail as this, just to get petted and coddled, right, Sergio?

\* \* \* \* \*

Inevitably—but then who would want to avoid it?—Salvador got me all dirty. In spite of a supposed desire not to confirm my predictions, Roxanna felt herself obligated to wash my pants, and so there was no other way out but to invite us to her apartment. I thought I knew very well how everything was going to turn out, and when I found myself alone with Sergio in her little sitting room, in my shorts (just as on the previous occasion, Roxanna wasn't embarrassed to see me like that), I resumed telling him what would happen.

At that stage I accepted the relative exactness of the coincidences as something beyond my control but, presuming I was aware of the intensity of the experiences that were approaching, I felt rather calm. Sergio never managed to understand anything. It seemed to him that if everything had already taken place (he was almost convinced of this) and if a series of events perhaps was going to be repeated more or less faithfully, then (above all, if he were to see himself involved in them) something was clearly lacking—so thought Sergio—in the absolute verisimilitude of the matter: he was a stranger to these events, for he had not been there the first time. Of course, he doubtless imagined them to be highly erotic at first, but eventually they turned out—given the ending which he was half aware of through the rumors that had not been lacking after that first time, since I myself had taken the trouble to propagate them—in the long run to be rather compromising. And that worried him. To find out whether it was more prudent to stay there or to run away before Roxanna came back with my pants, he asked me to give a quick rundown of what would happen next. Above all he wanted to know what part he was to play. His need for faith, in spite of all his hesitation, was impressive. I began by pointing out that I would tell him about the events just the way I would have finished telling them to him on the bus had not Roxanne appeared (reappeared?) with her dog. I wanted to make it clear that there were two things that did not coincide with the way they had happened the previous time. Besides the fact that he himself was definitely another person and not the fellow who had accompanied me on that other occasion, Roxanna herself was pretending to live these events for the first time. And this very conversation with Sergio, the explanations that I was on the point of offering him in the room filled with those posters of Lenin, Che, and Ho Chih Min that I knew so well, caused the context to change in a radical way, for my other friend had waited in silence, letting things follow their natural order, which of course at that time we were unaware of.

I don't deny that I myself began to get nervous just as I was telling Sergio that Roxanna would emerge from the bathroom with my pants in her hand and, startled to notice the extent of my excitement, would nevertheless stand there looking at me impudently, and then she would ask my friend to take off his pants too. I didn't want to go into details and I only suggested to Sergio the wantonness which would quickly spread throughout the room. Logically, I couldn't know whether things would turn out the same way, since Sergio had no reason to react like my other friend had done, nor she either to act the same way as before. If he took it into his head to be hesitant, if he got inhibited, things might take another direction. I thought this to be so obvious that I didn't try to comment on it. I did attempt to work some enthusiasm into him, though. I wanted the night to continue faithful to the model I had evoked. It didn't turn out that way.

\* \* \* \* \*

Roxanna didn't look at Raymundo lustfully but with astonishment. "Get yourself dressed, get dressed right now," she screamed at him. "But you're supposed to get excited when you see me," he exclaimed ridiculously. "You have to ask my friend to take his pants down, too. And then you take off your blouse, you come up to Sergio and I come over to the both of you and . . . Why do you pretend you don't remember?" Raymundo added brusquely while he took hold of her arm. "Get out of here, you beasts!" Roxanna was screaming again. "You're mad." She had thrown his wet pants in his face and now she went to open the door to the hallway, wide open. "Get out of here, you bastards!" she screamed again like a maniac. Salvador, who had been sitting all that time on the sofa (just like that other time, according to Raymundo), howled and tried to bite me on the foot. I panicked and was the first one to get out. Raymundo followed me. But first, as he was putting on his pants, he thanked her for washing them for him. "I didn't want to offend you, I swear . . . But everything was happening just the same as it did a year ago, everything, even down to the fact that I know I have been here, that I know you, Roxanna, or at least that once in a room identical to this one we made love in a threesome, and someone who otherwise must have been your twin, was wonderfully insatiable, fabulous!" Then Roxanna slapped him. I was watching from the doorway, inwardly making fun of Raymundo a little. The clatter of the door slamming shut imposed a heavy silence on us that was to last until we reached my house.

\* \* \* \* \*

You and your "strange things," Raymundo; confess at least that you invented the business about things repeating themselves. The fact is that it was I who pointed out to you that the girl and the dog had suddenly come up to us at the very moment you were telling me that this had happened once before. But then after that undeniable coincidence, you invented the rest. Yes, my friend, don't deny it, it was only after she told you her name that you pretended that you knew it. All right, agreed, you were able to tell her the name of her dog, another surprising coincidence that allowed you precisely to pique her curiosity and get her to follow along. Besides, let me tell you, that Chihuahua had the kind of face that couldn't have any other name except Salvador, even I would have hit on that. And then, taking advantage of your experience on heaven knows what other occasion (probably you even invented it, foreseeing the possibility that you might be able to induce it to happen; knowing you as I do, it wouldn't be too far out to suppose so), you suggested to the girl the bit about carrying the dog. And of course, during the long trip, with all the heat and its not being able to move, the poor animal did shit on you. Things became linked together little by little in a certain way under your clever direction, and since you yourself had spoken about getting your pants washed when you mentioned that other story, the poor girl, in her embarrassment, had no other choice but to offer to wash them for you. The rest of it, including that cheeky way she had of asking you to take off your pants right there, that wasn't too unexpected. Because from the outset we knew we were dealing with a rather liberated sort of girl, didn't we? Nevertheless you saw what happened then. Your ingenuity got out of control. Her reaction to your crudeness was so authentic and so violent that it was able to do more than you could. Confess, Raymundo, you lost it. All right, it's OK, you don't accept it. It's all the same to me. What I want to know is what really happened to you that other time. As we were walking in the rain you mentioned a kind of subtle conspiracy that you didn't want to complain about, one that was concocted so as to involve you, and also some sort of astonishment that comes over you upon recalling the events of that strange experience just as if they were happening again. Because I am beginning to suspect that the bits and pieces of the story you related to me while we were waiting in her sitting room were nothing more than some kind of anticipation of what you would have liked to see happening there. Don't keep silent, don't invent any more, just tell me the truth.

\* \* \* \* \*

All right then, Sergio, what really happened was that after a long night of alcohol and outrageous sex, each of us taking turns with the girl several times, we were confronted with an unexpected interruption. Someone had called the police and they broke into the apartment by knocking down the door. They caught Roxanna and my friend. I jumped out the window and ran, oh, I don't know how many blocks, all in my bare skin, to the astonishment of the few people who were walking around the streets at that hour. I finally managed to steal some pieces of curtain from a house that I found open and in this fashion, half covered, I took a taxi. Ever since then I have had the feeing—the need, to be more exact—that I would meet Roxanna again. Do you know why I wanted to relive all that, including the risk of such an ending? Because what I have been relating to you is nothing more than the synthesis of a story that I wrote years ago, and in that sense I have lived it over and over again. One does have fantasies, right? Crazy ideas it's not enough to have happen only in your imagination? I wanted to bring them into being by taking advantage of a chance event which this afternoon seemed made to measure, filling in the weak points. At any rate, I don't think we have wasted our time, at least I haven't. Now I know that Roxanna exists and that, yes, I have been to her house. By polishing up that story and blending it with what happened to us today, something interesting will probably come out of it, anyway. And maybe there will come a time, a deliciously ambiguous time, when I will no longer know whether she ran us out of her house accompanied by the sound of her screaming or, whether, with the taste of her crotch still in my mouth, I am still running through the streets so as not to get arrested for violating the canons of a virtuous life.

## the offering

Every night he stayed up writing until very late. Immersed in the world he was creating, he never felt the time passing. When he raised his head at last, the silence was his sweetest companion. He knew himself to be alone then, but in harmonious company. And he would go to sleep satisfied.

He awoke filled with energy, exuding enthusiasm. On his work table he kept going through the sheets of paper, one by one, breaking up the difficult meanings, revising ideas. Then he would take a long walk through the fields, filling his eyes and lungs with a lucidity that would be useful later on, when there was no longer any clarity in the doorways.

And then nightfall would arrive once more, and with it the intense explosion of images which were at once converted into complex networks of paths traced out in words. It was impossible to know where those paths were leading, but that didn't matter. He was capable of intuiting that his inspiration would eventually be depleted abruptly at the precise moment when he discovered the origin of his fervor or the destiny of his creations. And he would write for hours without stopping, as if driven by a mysterious force.

One day he had the unaccustomed feeling that the years were going by, and then he began to feel the weariness. The sheets now formed a large stack on the table. Up to that moment he had read every morning only what he had written the previous night. But that night he was not able to sleep with his normal calm. He recalled that children used to count sheep in order to arrive more quickly at the state of dream, and suddenly he found himself counting the sheets of paper that had remained stacked up in some stratum of his mind. He managed to get halfway through his task. Nightmares were straining about his bed, and they were like inconclusive ideas possessed of the raging of the seas. He felt hollow and pliant, lacking in will, like a raft adrift, he who had always been so restrained in his world made of energy. It was as if everything that he still needed to create were weakening him for the future in order to come forth without his assistance. A moment came when he felt himself so light that he was afraid of levitating, and in a panic he hastened to awaken.

The following morning he set himself to read from the beginning. The more he familiarized himself with his material, the more excessive and complex his elaboration seemed, considering the simplicity to which the theme could be reduced. And the more unusual ramifications he encountered in the concepts as well as in the language itself, the more he would tear apart, cross out, and compress as much as possible.

Thus the hours passed and he forgot to start on his usual walk through the fields. Nighttime surprised him scrutinizing labyrinthine scenes. He suspected that in reality everything that he wanted to add to the novel was already said in what he had written up to that point, and then he intensified the critical nature of his reading. When even with his eyes almost glued to the paper it became difficult for him to clarify certain passages, he first attributed his impotence to the gratuitous complexity they had acquired, and then to the progressive weariness of his eyes, without realizing that it was simply the growing darkness that was filling the room.

A little afterward he gave up, worn out. He woke early and without anything to eat he worked until the wee hours of the morning.

Foreseeing that he would soon finish polishing the arduous work of years, this time he remembered to light the lamp. And when, finally exhausted, he considered his work finished, he was unable to distinguish the new light that began to filter in through the window from that other more opaque light which was still emanating from his lamp.

With his eyes fixed on the final sentence, he read it aloud once more, trying to discover whether it really formed the right ending: *They all bent down their heads and immediately carried on with the ceremony, measuring in their primitive fashion the amount of time still wanting for the great cloud, watchful as a dragon, to speak out with its hoarse rattle and vomit fire and desolation as so many times before, as in the beginning.*

Then he had serious questions. And in order to throw light on them once and for all, despite his weariness he wanted to thrust himself anew into that world he had invented, which was now so plain, so little dense. But clarity was already making itself bothersome on his sweating face. He was too conscious of the light, of the momentary deception that this signified, too alienated from the real motive for the ceremony.

Without lifting his gaze to the skies he was breathing heavily. He wanted to absorb all the energy accumulated in that new morning; who knows how many remained? He thought of the ocean, that unchanging witness of history, immense and powerful, that surrounded the island. And once again he felt himself enclosed by a contagious silence, within and forever.

Experience, that something whose significance he never managed to understand but which weighed in his bones and was nourished by empty spaces in his memory, would suggest to him that this ambiguous peace carried a sordid, black hollow imprisoned in its heart like an omen of the clouds still far off. Now everything was an eternal present, a sketch of figures that gained obscure meaning in the sand and on the walls still remaining upright.

And one curious figure was repeated, a symbol that could be found in the shelters of every tribe, that joined their members together through a common, obsessive memory: an enormous, overwhelming mushroom, distantly humbling, which the huge waves undertook to erase every time it reappeared upon the sand.

The worst was to have the feeling that a collective past had existed which no one could recall, to know that they were cut off from any future by the insurmountable threat of those clouds that periodically rained death and destruction upon the ruins. If there really existed a relationship among them that permitted them to be warned of perils, this was limited to the common yearning for fishing, routine sexual desire, and the ceremonies that attempted to soften the wrath of God.

He was breathing hard once more, scratching about in his mind for recollections. He thought that since he was the oldest perhaps he was also the most lucid, the one with the fullest consciousness of the inherited desolation. And therefore he was thought of as a guide. But it was not pleasant to know himself the repository of a responsibility without solutions.

He visualized himself as a child, also drawing mushrooms in the sand. He vaguely recalled the inferno of sparks and dense smoke which enbosomed him one whole morning long as they suddenly began to ascend, framed by the television screens of the entire world a little before these became melted down. He conjured up the scene as an event that had actually happened, but it was impossible for him to specify whether in reality he had been the one who was that child witness. And to measure time? Now, whether he would or not, he was in the midst of the rubble on an island, living a life that he seemed always to have shared with the others.

He looked at the sky. Thick layers of clouds were slowly moving in and getting closer. Once more that ungovernable peril. He sought among his things for the enormous conch shell he had kept ever since he could remember. He brought it to his lips and began to blow. The wind carried the sound away and changed it into a languid echo behind the ruins.

The clouds have become pressed together above the surface of the earth when the others start to gather on the beach. The old men kneel down, forming a large circle. The women and children stay behind the old men. The adolescents then begin to dance in the center, accompanying their little leaps with guttural intonations. Suddenly all movement ceases. Everyone turns to watch the wise man approaching with measured step and head bent down.

They have made way for him respectfully, and he places himself in the middle of the circle. He looks at the adolescents facing him. He points with his index finger at a young girl, and she chooses her partner. While both are putting aside their scanty garments, everyone looks with terrorstricken eyes at the sky now stained with black. Shortly after, the couple on the sand, putting all their faith into it, slowly begins the first movements of the rite. And then, carried away by the same fervor, no one dares lift anew their eyes to the sky.

Watching them in their coupling, the wise man cannot understand why he feels himself summoned from some distant place. For an instant he has a familiar vision. As before in his dreams, he sees himself dressed in other clothing, seated before a curious apparataus which produces sharp sounds on contact with his finger. He is able to see, through other tired eyes, the minute signs which the apparatus keeps imprinting on a white surface which slips along laterally. Unable to place the vision, he closes his eyes in confusion.

The couple were already allowing the final spasms to escape to their feet when he separated them again. He lifted his eyes then; all lifted their eyes. The sky was now a single, compact, black cloud. Immediately he chose the next couple and, just as he had previously done, readied them for the consummation of the offering.

The all bent down their heads and immediately carried on with the ceremony, measuring in their primitive fashion the amount of time still wanting for the great cloud, watchful as a dragon, to speak out with its hoarse rattle and vomit fire and desolation as so many times before, as in the beginning.

# while he lay sleeping

Carlos awakened with difficulty after an unusual effort which, for the duration of a moment that was terrifyingly long, made him fear, still semiconscious, that he would never be able to awaken again. It had been a sensation of profound anguish, similar to what one goes through when struggling to have one more orgasm after many previous ones during a night of intense pleasure and wantonness. And now he was sweating in the darkness of the room. Warmth descended on him like a great viscous cloak. He recalled the immense bird that had fallen on his bed, enveloped in flames that lit up the infinite extension of the heavens. He saw himself burning again, screaming, and suddenly he felt the pain lacerating his flesh. When he succeeded finally in returning the anguish to the plane where it belonged, to the exact dimension of the dream, paroxisms of water were streaming down over him. He had run to the bathroom and was now under the shower.

His urine, an intense yellow, was vacating his bladder now in a long, interminable jet. His penis was losing its stiffness little by little, allowing him to draw nearer and nearer the toilet bowl. There are people who have an erection when faced with the idea of death, he thought. Years before, he had had a lover who would arouse herself by associating the final moment of her life with the most intense sexual climax that could be felt. And afterward, that very unusual woman used to say, there would come a dream equally profound, delicious, without any feeling of time limits because she had to get up at a certain time to go to work.

Thinking that if she had been a man she would have spent the best part of her life with a hard on, Carlos observed himself carefully in the mirror of the medicine cabinet. He was a little swollen around the eyes, his hair was jumbled and his beard thick. The bitter taste that felt doughy in his mouth bothered him, and taking a little water in the palm of his hand, he sucked it up only to spit it out with disgust afterward. He didn't wash his face because he still wanted to sleep. There was no reason for the nightmare to be repeated.

He cannot sleep. He lights a cigarette. Strange how now it doesn't bother him to smoke. Before, when he was eighteen and spent his time in training, the only thing that interested him was keeping himself always in shape. Angélica, his first girl friend, used to come to watch him afternoons working out in the garage. She was seventeen then, and had magnificent breasts which according to what she told him were the envy of all her girl friends.

Squatting beneath a bar with two hundred pounds on his shoulders after having done that odious exercise for his legs nine times, he is just about to rise once more when Angélica suddenly comes into the garage sporting a pair of very tight shorts. The surprise and his exhaustion come together to cause his legs to tremble and him to lose his balance. Sensing that he is going over forward, with a great effort he lets loose of the bar. It bounces against his heel. The pain is horrible. Angélica, motionless in front of him, doesn't know whether to laugh or scream out in pity. Leaning on her, he succeeds a little later in getting as far as the house. Although his foot is a great shapeless mass and the pain is pulling tears from his eyes, he manages to hold back his moaning. "Women are a lot braver than men," his girl friend had told him some days before, and he had nearly died laughing. "I know it hurts you, Carlos. For Heaven's sake forget our bet and let yourself

*while he lay sleeping* 63

groan if you have to," the girl begs him now time and time again, but Carlos only shakes his head.

On another occasion, he remembers while taking out a new cigarette, Angélica was watching him work his abdominals on the inclined bench. They had been going together only a few months then, and he had not dared to get too far with her. French kissing, as it used to be called then, was their most daring thing. Standing next to his feet, which were on the raised part of the bench and tied down with a leather strap, Angélica was counting out loud. He raised and lowered his trunk with his hands clasped behind his neck, trying not to pay too much attention to her so as not to lose his concentration.

He is getting tired and is starting to look at her from below while rising slower and and slower each time. How beautiful her tits look from that angle, so tightly fit into her sweater. He cannot go on with the exercise because his penis, erect beneath his bathing suit, has gotten the girl's attention and she, blushing furiously, has had to withdraw to one side of the garage.

He is close to her now and is excited even more upon noticing how her breasts are rising and falling because of her nervousness. She tries not to look at him, she says not a word. Then Carlos, without thinking what he is doing, brusquely pulls down the zipper, revealing that part of her breasts not covered by the skimpy bra. As he separates them from the fabric with his avid hands, he feels the girl's slight trembling transmitted to his fingers.

He sees her breasts for the first time, whiter and smaller than he had imagined them, two beautiful pears without the peel. Grasping her firmly by the shoulders, he pushes her down. When both are on their knees, he lowers his lips to one flustered breast and is pleasantly surprised to feel how rigid her nipple is. He puts his girl friend's cool hand inside his bathing suit then and makes her close her fingers over his penis. Wondering which must was the most aroused, his cock or that small breast which he was sucking on so enthusiastically, he slips his hand down until he feels Angélica's moistness and begins to rub.

Upon looking at her, he sees that his girl friend is weeping silently. He withdraws his hand and makes her do the same. He helps her to stand up and afterward to put her clothing in order. "See you tomorrow," Angélica says just before leaving, when Carlos is about to ask her pardon. Both are pale. "All right," he responds. He watches her depart and afterwards goes back into the garage and closes the door from inside. Stretched out on the narrow bench, he brings to mind the photos of the most recent Playboy that he keeps in a box next to his bed and he masturbates without rushing, substituting Angélica's face for that of the model, until reaching plenitude. Then he remains asleep on the bench, on the bed now, with cigarette still lit.

An enormous bird, still far off, begins to descend once more upon the sleeping body. Enveloped in flames it penetrates the precinct of the mind that is dreaming it. The heat becomes the more intense the more swiftly that great burning mass comes down. The fire makes contact with the flesh. It devours it in dreams and consumes the body stretched out upon the bed. The room is burning, the whole house is burning, but Carlos cannot situate that real fire because he continues thinking himself in that garage where he does his exercises every day. He has awakened there and interprets this strange dream as a simple foretaste of the passion he is to reach in his future relationship with Angélica. He smiles, thinking that instead of a girl friend he will soon have a lover, a charming seventeen-year-old lover whom he will go on molding in accord with his desires and caprices because everything gives way before fire: the house now, the room before that, he himself a second ago without his even managing to wake up.

# the reader

*For Carlos Fuentes*

i

Here is the rocking chair, there the sofa bed, toward the rear the mahogany desk. Isabel is rocking; her sister is dozing stretched out beneath a heavy blanket; I am reading, seated with my back to both of them. Outside, the rain insists on flooding the still dark garden. The wind launches gusts of water against the glass. No one pays any attention to the storm. The sisters because they are now accustomed to it; apparently they have been living here for years. He, because he is coming across scenes every minute that he would never have imagined and so does not raise his eyes from the book that was handed him hours earlier.

The oldest is about thirty years of age; she is very thin and looks to be about fifty. Her grayish hair has not made acquaintance with a comb for heaven knows how long, perhaps not that of a hand either, not even her own hand. But her eyes, which remain beautiful amid the incipient wrinkles, are clear, and they seem to light up when the rocker moves forward bringing her serene face toward the light bulb that hangs from the ceiling and weakly illuminates the room. From time to time she smiles without being aware of it. She is probably remembering the now remote occasion when someone told her that Isabel was a lovely name but that her eyes were even lovelier, like a sad doll's. Still, it would be difficult to really know her thoughts. She herself is unaware that she has any.

Veronica is about to round out twenty years of age, and her hair is very long and black. She has a beautiful body, and she has known it since those days when the sweaty hands first used to feel her up in the darkness. She is also aware of how repulsive her face is. She would like to be the owner of lovely eyes like her sister's. She would be ready any time to give up her youthful body in exchange for those eyes. But that is impossible. She will remain cross-eyed forever. There is only one way to repair her defect: an operation. But it costs a lot of money. And she will never accept the advice that her dreams suggest. She will never be the prostitute that she is in the chillingly clear scene in the book which she has given Vincent to read and which she perhaps is dreaming at this very moment.

Vincent, of course, is I. He is the one reading so attentively, unprecedentedly for him, soaking up the incredible things narrated in the novel that Veronica has urged on him. He doesn't know why the girl had insisted so much, but that was why he had come: to read, and now he is not sorry to have begun this reading out loud but in a low voice, just as he was bidden, and without asking questions about the reason for this apparently useless activity.

All the things the girl in the book does to get money together, the graphic way each incident is described, every thought stained with a dark rancor, turn out to be strangely fascinating for him and totally alien to his experience. Other parts of the book, on the other hand, seem incongruous, lacking the most elemental anecdotal cohesiveness, sometimes even vague. What has all this got to do with me, he asks himself at the end of every paragraph. Do they think maybe that I have enough culture to be able to discuss the book with them afterwards, to offer some critical remarks like those that come out in the newspapers sometimes? And he goes on reading, allowing himself to be carried along by a childish curiosity just as when he was going to school, but nonetheless perceiving the hallucinatory absence of fluidity in the telling, sensing that there are some chunks of it drawn from nightmares and others that only a defective mind could have put in, and that by main force. But none of this is important to him because his work consists in reading and not in asking questions.

Vincent is unaware that from here, next to Isabel's rocking chair, I am contemplating the nearly perfect immobility of his posture. Isabel and Veronica are not aware of it either. If they were ever to suspect it, what is happening this rainy night in Noloc would never have taken place, and what is more, I would not be here. But not to anticipate events. Let it suffice for the moment to know that it will be two more hours before they actually take place; I have gotten out of time and am now installed in it again, but from another perspective, looking at what still hasn't happened yet, a perspective that permits me unendingly this willed retrocession. The rain continues to come down. The wind, just as it must be doing there at my own house where my wife is busy and the child is crying, never ceases to throw water against the window panes.

ii

I was made a woman at fourteen, by force. I had always thought people only looked on me as a being with deformed eyes which caught their attention, of course, but immediately brought forth gibes, pity, or an effort to maintain an indifferent attitude. If my mirror has always given me back the true image of my face ever since my childhood, that is because mirrors cannot alter reality either, though some people manage to believe the contrary, due to their powerful imaginations which rearrange images and compensate for empty spaces. Thanks to my daily encounter with myself I had become resigned. But one day I stopped wearying myself with the always identical expression of my crossed eyes looking-at-me look-at-them looking-at-me look-at-them because I discovered how my skinny body was mysteriously filling out. I was reborn in the delicious fusion of the tactile with the visual.

Men realized this at the same time and began to smile at me. I felt happy. I allowed them to follow me any old time through the puddled streets of Noloc. The first hand that felt my buttocks was too rough, but it awakened unsuspected resonances in me. And when something pleases us or comforts us we allow our eagerness for it to gratify us amply. Therefore I didn't object to their fondling me in the dark hallways, beneath the stairs, in the farthest corners of the movie houses. Until one time they wanted me to go all the way, and it occurred to me to set as a condition that they would have to look steadily at my eyes for five minutes.

There were three fellows after me. Since they were such good friends among themselves, they wanted to share me. I told them they could all have me after each one had first complied with my conditions. I wanted to feel that I was getting something in exchange, even though it only meant a very small sacrifice for them. On other occasions they had pawed me over without once resting their gaze on my face.

They agreed, but laughing insanely. They wanted me to take off my clothes first. I said no. First they were to look at my eyes for five minutes, each one of them, or no go. The bastards blindfolded me with an enormous piece of cloth, tied my hands with another, and then ripped my skirt off. They had forgotten to put a gag on me, and I screamed in rage. A rag that turned out to be a piece of my own blouse quickly stopped that, and then I could prevent nothing.

### iii

I don't know why it is that when you know what is going to happen, the minutes acquire an irritating, oppressive doughiness. Even though you know that Isabel will get up suddenly and without a second thought will move over to where her sister is lying, perhaps dreaming, as in the book, of accumulating more and more money because her capitulations never end, in spite of her exhaustion. Even though you know the reaction Veronica will have when she feels herself jostled around with malevolent brusqueness. Even though it is inevitable the Vincent should turn around in startlement upon hearing the girl's terrifying scream and be unable to believe that he is really hearing something that should lack all sound because it is only a literary description of the reaction of a character in the book that is in his hands. And although you know that this all takes place foreknown because it has already happened, now the events seem deliberately to postpone their realization, just to make my waiting all the more anguished. It's not for nothing that my wife says that everything that occurs in this world is a caprice of Time.

iv

I am very worried because Vincent left here more than eight hours ago and he still hasn't returned, he hasn't even called as he usually does when he decides to go for a drink with his few friends or if he gets interested in something else, even just going to a whorehouse until his bad mood goes away, and of course he never tells me he's really going to a whorehouse but he invents an excuse no matter how unlikely it comes out, so that I will know he is all right and not to worry, because the truth is that Vincent has always been very considerate toward me in that way, since no matter how serious our situation gets he never neglects to let me know that he is coming back late, well, yes, once he told me I'm going to a hotel to sleep, I'm sick of your complaining every night when I come home tired and need to sleep in peace, but the fact is that he did let me know he wasn't coming, he knows that I worry about everything and then I can't sleep and I get more neurotic than I usually am, especially just recently because of this damned pregnancy, and it's not that I don't like children, I love them, but my nerves have been so bad since my mother's death that I don't feel ready to have another baby, but God alone knows the happiness we felt when little Vincent was born, his father seemed like a child that someone had given an expensive toy to, he spent hours looking into his son's big black eyes and caressing his spongy skin, and I even had to get mad at him sometimes and ask him to leave the baby alone, and now, when I feel least capable of being able to face up to the responsibility of another long wait, I'm pregnant again, it makes me really angry, all from having paid attention to Father Benjamin and his "natural" rhythm method, the son of a bitch, with as easy as it would have been to swallow a little pill every night and that would take care of it, but no, come off it!, the Blessed Mother Church does not look kindly upon all these newfangled artificial devices that the market is so full of these days, my daughter, and that's all there is to it, and that's why it seems so strange to me that Vincent hasn't even called the neighbor's house as he always does when he's going to come back late, besides, the argument we had wasn't any more intense than the other ones recently, the worst is that the poor guy goes around so worried about getting work, every day he buys several newspapers and starts circling every ad that interests him, except that when he arrives at the appointed place it turns out that they require I don't know how many years of schooling or some stupid letters of recommendation or a certain age, and if they were going to set up so many dumb obstacles and conditions why in hell couldn't they say so in the ad from the beginning, I don't know why it matters that he didn't finish school, he found out how to educate himself and that's worth more, and besides, how do they expect him to get letters of recommendation if it's only been a few months since we came to Noloc and we still don't know anyone important? although no one doubts that we're honest people, it's only a question of trying us out, as Vincent says, but they just don't want to, and as far as his age goes, he is rather young, yes, but he's not afraid of work, he would do anything that didn't go against his principles, because one thing is certain, I can get jealous over him sometimes and get mad at him for things when I suspect that he is getting involved with other women, and I even call him a son of a bitch from time to time, of course, because that's the way I am and I don't let myself go on like the others, but I'll always stand behind him for his high ideals and his humility and companionship, he is a wonderful father and as a lover the truth is, I don't think anyone is complaining around here, oh Blessed Virgin Mary, right now I want him to come home with his big, strong hands and start fondling my neck very slowly while he says to me, keep taking your clothes off, woman, because I've got a tremendous urge to hump you, and then I feel him hard against my thigh and afterward he picks me up and lays me down on the bed just like on our wedding night, only that time he was too drunk and couldn't do anything with me, the poor guy, but I do know that if he were to see me now with my breasts quivering waiting for his lips he would start taking off his shirt without stopping kissing me and then his pants and finally his socks, and my body would be waiting for him forgetful of the being that has been forming within it ever since once when the same kind of impulse shot the hell out of that rhythm method, and we'd be enjoying ourselves now as so many other times, just happy to be together, trying to forget that little Vincent is crying where we left him in his crib in the corner, crying because he needs the breast that his father has deprived him of.

V

Veronica feels herself shaken out of her dream because her sister is already next to her, jerking her around violently. Flabbergasted, Vincent hears the girl's rending shriek, as it was foreseen that he would hear it, and he whirls around in time to see how Isabel is sinking her nails into the younger girl's body and how the latter, defending herself, scratches at Isabel's eyes. Their blood is becoming a great pool that is spreading everywhere.

Vincent runs to pull them apart, and he finally manages. Veronica's breasts are dripping. Isabel's torn eyes are flowing with blood. He looks in fright from one to the other and has an urge to get out of this nightmare, to go out into the rain and run until he can reach his own house and feel that there he can understand what is going on because there is a certain enchantment in routine and in seeing his wife's swollen belly and not being able to sleep because of little Vincent's crying.

Suddenly he recalls that it was only this morning when he had opened the newspaper to the classifieds and had been overjoyed to find that a reader was wanted at a certain house. Eager to find out what the situation was, although he assumed that it would only be a matter of reading over the news to some old blind woman, he set his steps toward the place where he is now. When she opened the door, Isabel smiled at him as if she had known him all her life and immediately stepped aside. Veronica was waiting for him with the novel in her hand, housecoat open to the waist. Her heavy black hair flowing over her shoulders and breasts did not completely hide her lines. It surprised him when she insisted on his sitting down to read right then, without raising his voice nor paying any attention to the two sisters while he was doing it, but this did not prevent the required decision. He had managed stranger tasks. Before Veronica went back toward the weakly illuminated rear of the room, she assured him that the contents of the book were a reflection of life and that he would eventually see that for himself. Vincent didn't understand what this had to do with anything, but at that point she drew away, and he immediately sat down to read. Now, standing in front of the two sisters who, though battered, were smiling as if nothing had happened, he recalls that he should turn his back on them and knows that he must return to his reading; that is the only way to understand.

### vi

I don't pretend to say I didn't enjoy what they did to me that afternoon, it was something I have never felt since. But the hatred that was born at the same time also remains in me like a calcium deposit that makes my bones feel enormously heavy.

Every time they look at me going by on my way to school, I know they think she is easy and now she's just trying to turn us on with her fake indifference. I don't care. They must have been thinking that for a couple of years now, because something prevents them from approaching me as they used to before. They don't even dare say anything to me as I go by. My sister says that with the body I have I should always be surrounded by men; she doesn't understand why they have stopped besieging me. I am certain that at bottom my newfound solitude pleases her because this way we have something in common and by sharing it we can suppress our envy. What Isabel is unaware of is that I give the impression of deep-seated scorn, which men perceive and which frightens them. Now they look at my eyes from a distance, but with a different bearing, without smiling in that jeering way. Some day I will neutralize my feelings for long enough to give myself the pleasure of hearing them scream as I could not do that time under the initial pain. But on the other hand, no man will ever be able to enjoy it as much as I did, in spite of myself, while they were humiliating me. Day by day I think more and more. I am constructing my life on the basis of the plans I keep making, and I build my plans on the patient monotony of my life. So as not to forget anything, so as not to allow anything to go unaccomplished, I write everything down with my typewriter on these pages which some day I will have bound into a single volume so it will seem like a unique little book. And every man that wants to get near me will have to make the things that I have described his own through reading about them. They of course will expect me to recompense them at the end for such a prolonged and absurd labor. Whoever manages to get to the final line will have met with a destiny that at first was only a vague idea in my head.

### vii

Since they do not answer Vincent when he asks again if he should call a doctor, if he might do anything for them, he inquires about the reason for the battle. The blood gushing from both women, who are now watching him impassively, is more real than the possibility that they might offer anything in response. That's the way he understands it, and therefore he exclaims, "Do I go on reading? It's not much longer now, that's what you hired me for."

Their silence causes him to recall that they have never once spoken about money at all, he almost doesn't know what he is doing here, only that he was told to read on until the end. He feels tempted to ask how much they will pay him, or whether they would like an opinion about the book. He tells himself they will surely explain everything to him afterwards, doubtless it will be the cross-eyed one with the tempting breasts which are now shamelessly in front of him, at the height of his own chest, bloody, almost asking to be washed. She is tall, he hadn't noticed that before, because when he got there she had seemed to be hinting at something to him as she bent down lightly and unnecessarily toward him to hand him the book, as in a brief ceremony. All right then, let's see what happens, he thinks with a shake of his shoulders, and walks resolutely back to the desk.

viii

It's been nine hours since Vincent left and now I'm really getting afraid because it's six-thirty in the evening, and it keeps on raining and everything is so dark and deserted, as if it were the middle of the night with just a few hours to go before dawn, and the fact is that I don't know if I should call the police, because if I do it and Vincent were to appear suddenly as if nothing were wrong and give me some old excuse and then find out that I told them he was missing he may get mad at me and leave again, and I wouldn't be able to bear this loneliness any longer, nor little Vincent's crying for me to give him the breast, the way the little wretch is making me do even now, since he's actually started screaming again, he can't understand that I'm crying too, that I need his father, that I need him so much and I'd give anything to see him come in that door suddenly and say to me with a smile, Hi, you gorgeous doll, and perhaps he might even say, I've got a job, how does that look to you? before his oh so strong hands start to run delicately over my neck and his lips whisper, let's go to bed, and for the first time I wouldn't care about making love in front of the baby because I would think he has to learn some day.

ix

He is sitting again. He picks up the open book and recognizes the scene between the sisters that he has just witnessed, he recognizes having asked them if he might be useful to them. He turns back, looks for the precise line where the girl screams, and he confirms that what he has lived through is exactly what occurs in the book until he gets to the new paragraph which he is reading now and which says, "A scream was heard."

But this time he realizes that he is not only really hearing the scream but that he is also feeling it, since it is he who is screaming from the pain produced by the knife that has pierced his lung with a single movement.

# ALIENATIONS

## the shoes

It continues to rain. The sound of the waves diminishes. The moon has disappeared. Along the coast behind some dark rocks the tent has fused with the immense, boundless night.

As if he did not exist. As if the one walking toward the place that had previously been illuminated did not exist either. What is it, then, that he is approaching? And who is it moving along so slowly, treading on a sandy beach that his feet no longer feel? Someone, evidently, is thinking this. Doubts do not arise from nothing. Unless the emptiness is secretly alive and capable of perceiving the point to which the silence has been turning into enormous darkness in every remote little spot.

He has reached it. Where the tent had been he finds a pair of shoes. He picks them up. Turns them over. A fine white dust falls on the dark sand and forms a broken star at his feet.

The moment he recognizes the shoes as his own, he realizes he is barefoot. Only now he feels the warmth of the sand, the suffocation of this night that lacks all reference points. He exists, then, but he is alone.

In his hands there remains the sensation of the weight which the shoes had had just a moment ago, the ones he has on now. He doesn't recall having removed his clothes and nonetheless there they are, at his feet. Once more he hears the murmuring of the waves.

The tent is behind him when he ceases searching the ocean with his eyes. But the moon, which is throwing a pale light on his skin stretched out beside his clothes on the sand, scatters no light upon the skeleton that remains on its feet in bewilderment, wearing the shoes.

# as if there were nothing the matter

a park. A balloon man approaches. She gets up from the bench where she has been absentmindedly contemplating the pigeons pecking about at her feet. She has heard the pleasant jingling that seems to float toward her. She sees how the man is intercepted a few yards away by three naked girls, radiant with joy, who have run out from the thick underbrush along the path. Their white bodies shine like sword blades in the sun and a glittering breaks away from their long blond hair, all of which produces the effect of a cutting brightness about them, forcing her to lower her eyes.

Shading her eyes with her hand then, she realizes that the girls are asking the wandering peddler for balloons, for the latter hands one to each of them. Immediately they lose themselves in the shrubbery, jumping like little children. She still manages to see over the tops of the bushes the slow red, blue, and white rocking movements of the balloons drawing away. She also wants to have a lovely balloon so she can run along with it against the wind. She offers a coin to the balloon man. Unable to catch a glimpse of the head hidden behind the balloons, which are tied to very short lines, she hears a voice that says, "All the ones I have left are reserved." She feels a sudden urge to cry. The moment she makes up her mind just to grab one and run, the other hand thrusts out suddenly in front of her holding the only one she can have: a flattened little balloon in a milky white color. She asks the man to blow it up. The latter responds that it is impossible, he is very tired because he has just finished blowing up all the others. The young woman thinks, "Nothing ever comes out for me," but she is pleased anyway with the idea of possessing one of her very own, so she deposits the coin in the palm of that anonymous hand, takes the balloon, and walks away.

Seated on the bench, she delicately applies her lips to the rubber neck and begins to blow. Nothing. Her face gets purple and the veins stand out on her neck. Siezed with great longing, she moves her head around in spirals while she continues blowing with all her might. She notices vaguely that she too has become naked with the effort. She pays no attention to the people who gather around her with avid eyes. When the balloon finally begins to swell up, she feels a profound joy reddening her skin, which makes everyone applaud with satisfaction. She is sweating. Little by little the rubber has been filling out, becoming rigid. Suddenly, with any reason, the balloon deflates. It hangs limp from her exhausted lips.

After a moment of frustration, she again blows and blows, determined not to come off second best now that she recalls how the three girls had run off so happily. She manages at last to bring it up to the same size as before.

The bursting scorches her face and the white pieces fall over her legs like snowflakes. A sudden coldness takes possession of her senses and pierces her soul, causing her to fall sideways over her shadow. The curious onlookers run up shrieking to paw over her. Finally they get tired of that and all go off on their own. A little boy approaches. Full of curiosity, he pulls her legs apart, gives a shout, and runs away.

Tania awakens in a fright, with the feeling that that awful explosion is still burning her face. She lights the lamp. Eleven. But

*as if there were nothing the matter* 79

why is my face really burning? She runs to the mirror. There are no marks. Of course, there couldn't be any, though she is quite pale. Like the little white balloon. The one that she is unable blow up any more. The one that will never be hers because it was not hers to begin with. The exhaustion that her husband brings home with him every night also comes from pleasures that are not hers. And then he turns his back on me in bed and goes to sleep.

One night she had surprised him masturbating in his dreams. "Don't go away, Susan!" he was babbling. And then she perceived something different on her husband's body, like an emanation coming from his muscular back. The effluvium took shape while it was moving away, the classic form of a woman, sometimes phosphorescent, sometimes opaque. And disappeared. When she managed to get to sleep hours later, she dreamed of an amorphous face enveloped in long reddish hair. Some hairy hands broke out of the darkness and offered her a bloody fetus.

She opens her pajama top angrily. Her breasts are full and round, a temptation for the most exacting mouth. She is still beautiful. If she weren't a woman she would find herself desirable. Why are they playing such filthy tricks on me? "It's very simple," her husband had told her one night, "I don't love you. And without love, desire ends up falsified too." When he spoke to her in that way, she recalls as she buttons up again, she felt real hatred. An intense, dangerous hatred that made my hand instinctively light on the scissors on top of the chest of drawers. The cold of the steel brought me around, just in time. She got dressed and went out for a walk, eager to revenge herself in any way possible. That night she would have offered herself to any man on the street in exchange for a little tenderness, even if it were only verbal. But the street was deserted. It was raining. She walked without any fixed direction; how long? The dampness penetrated her flesh with delight, settled in her bones. She began to sneeze but kept on walking. It had stopped raining and the sun was showing feebly from behind an opaque gray when I got back home. He was snoring as usual. That very afternoon the chills began to shake me. I was burning with fever. I woke up in the hospital. "It's nothing," my husband said when he saw me come to, "just simple pneumonia. You'll get over it."

Now he is snoring again beside her, his back turned. At three in the morning, she had perceived a slight noise at the street door just as she was falling off. She knew it was he when she heard him cough. She remained quiet in the darkness, on the lookout. She sensed him steering toward the bathroom on tip toe, carefully shutting the door. Immediately the prolonged sound of the water rushing through the toilet reached her. He came out in his shorts and slipped under the bedclothes. The smell of alcohol brought on a muffled rage in her, sharper than it did other times. But it is his snoring that rubs at Tania's nerves now; the repeated indifference of that broad back offends her, denies her.

A few nights ago when she had started to hang his pants on a hanger, she had noticed a little red box that had fallen from his pocket. She picked it up from the floor and confirmed her suspicion. The week before, she had found an eyebrow pencil in his inside coat pocket. She hadn't said anything to him on that occasion. What would she have gained by that? More discussions? For a long time it was no secret that her husband had extramarital relations. But who with? That night she couldn't hold back her anger, and when he was standing before her on the verge of offering a new excuse for his tardiness, Tania showed him the little box. He grew pale. He said, I always take them with me just in case; I'm not a queer and if any woman offers herself to me I'm not going to tell her no thanks, the fact is I'm married and I respect my wife too much. And why should you expose yourself to venereal diseases in situations like that, he argued.

"In spite of everything I do love you, but I've never tried to deny that other women attract me very easily."

"All right, but what about me?"

No response.

"Answer me, please."

"What do you want me to tell you? You're my wife. I do it with you every night. But sometimes one gets a little bored."

"Oh, variety!"

"It's useless to talk about these things with one's wife. You wouldn't be able to understand."

"I understand perfectly. Who is your lover?"

"I don't have a lover."

"Tell that to your mother!"

"I've told you before, don't you mention my mother when we're *as if there were nothing the matter*

arguing, you cunt!"
"Why not? You're fascinated by whores, aren't you?"
"Shut up!"
"I won't shut up."
"I said, shut your mouth! Now!"

And he tore into my mouth with a slap, recalled Tania. This goat of a husband hit me on the mouth! And now he's sleeping so calmly, he snores as if there were nothing the matter, smells up the room with his breath, stores up energies he wastes in other arms . . . bowled over by the novelty of the other sex, excited by a different perfume, by gasps with a different rhythm . . . Damn! And I just go on loving him!

". . . and you cannot sleep without screwing off the top of the pill jar and swallowing one in which the ordering of the world has been condensed, chemically pure," says Rosario Castellanos in a poem that Tania has read somewhere and now remembers, conscious of her insomnia. She searches for the bottle of pills in the darkness, which has become clearer in the bedroom but more and more intensified in her head the more aware she is that an idea which has just come into her mind is becoming less remote, more firm. Her hand gropes for the glass of water after an abrupt motion has already shoved a fistfull of pills into her mouth. She brings the glass to her lips and swallows, swallows again, until the water is finished.

She closes her eyes and the darkness becomes perfect, quite suited to the one that is coming, entirely befitting the reality that has clung to her marriage from the beginning. Anyway, he'll go to work in the morning without realizing anything. I will be the body that goes on sleeping, searching for evasion in sleep. The mannequin of his wife. But I will have already ceased being that. Perhaps I'll be something else, a variation, a shadow . . . or nothing at all.

## oscillations

He is very hungry. The emptiness gnawing at his insides obliges him to curl up. He begins to feel cold and unable to control the shivering of his body as his temperature goes lower. To protect himself from the cold he moves into the fetal position. He tells himself over and over that the heat is unbearable and he has eaten too much. So great is the feeling of bloated satiation distending his belly that he assumes a vertical position once more in order to adjust to this new annoyance. He does not hold up under the stiflment that draws thick drops of sweat to his flushed skin, and he tosses his clothes to the floor. But the icy currents that arrive unexpectedly and embed themselves in the marrow of his bones force him to double over again until he becomes a compact, trembling ball. Then the hunger returns, to drive him crazy. First he bites off the fingers of one hand and swallows them one by one. Then he devours the other hand. Arms and feet follow, making an abstraction out of pain until it is turned into unbounded delight. Having had his fill of flesh, he feels a savage warmth that courses through his veins with an infinite number of needle pricks. Using his teeth he opens fissures in his remaining skin, trying to cool himself down by contact with the air. Cold comes in, a chill which turns his blood into floes harder than his bones.

# underwood

The letter had been delayed. Now he was holding it before his eyes, folded open but furrowed between his fingers. He hadn't managed to begin reading it. The characters were blurry, the words fused together as if tears had been dripping on them. But he wasn't weeping. It had been a long time since he had given himself that satisfaction. To the contrary he was hestitant, uneasy about the reply he had been secretly expecting for what seemed like a lifetime. He concentrated, making an immense effort, and the individual letters gradually recovered their little shapes with the small, sharp separations that characterized the portable Underwood he himself had bought a little after the wedding.

The whole contents could be summed up in the final line: I STILL LOVE YOU. I'LL ARRIVE ON FRIDAY.

He crumpled the page. Almost immediately he straightened it out again. His eyes ran eagerly over the apologies, the pleas, the outlines of her plans for things they would do together. Everything had been her fault, she assured him. But it would never happen again. Then came the reaffirmation of what he had prayed for every night.

And finally the simple announcement of her arrival. As he looked to see what time it was, he noted with astonishment that it was already Friday. He ran to his car already anticipating her embrace, feeling her repentance, her shame, against his body. It was just dawn.

He waited long hours at the station. His thoughts were lost in the most involved conjectures. He recalled suddenly that he didn't know what time she would arrive. Nor even how she would be travelling. She might even come on a plane; that wouldn't be unusual. Then why was he at the bus depot, waiting for who knows what bus? He had driven there without giving it any thought at all, perhaps guided by the form taken so many times by that dream. He always saw her getting off smiling, her eyes searching for him, until she saw him standing next to the column that was now holding him up. He told himself in disgust that he was an imbecile.

Fortunately he had the letter with him. Hastily he unfolded it. There was no indication of how she would get herself to the city. Several minutes passed, and his uncertainty was becoming more dense. Why hadn't it occurred to her to explain the time and place of her arrival clearly? She hadn't changed. Just as irresponsible as always. She will have to take a taxi to the house because he can't do anything more now. He would wait for her there.

Night came on dense and agonizing. It didn't help at all during the day to read the newspapers around him. Neither was he distracted by listening to the radio or going out on the balcony every little while. It would be midnight soon and then the arrival of Saturday would take on the task of proving once again what he always suspected: she was a liar, the cruelest of cheats.

At one in the morning he pledged never to believe a single word of hers again. Even if a thousand letters came, begging his pardon, or if he were to hear her supplicating voice on the phone.

He walked to the little Underwood, put a sheet in, and typed quickly. The words came out weak, faded. He changed the ribbon and wrote:

Dear Ramiro,

You really must pardon me. I missed the plane on Friday. I will come next week without fail. I'll let you know. I love you. You must believe me . . .

## the first meeting

He was a lonely patrician. The first time he became aware of his lack of friends, he had already inherited an immense fortune. The exact particulars which permitted him to benefit in such a fashion from the death of that relative were unknown to him, but he never allowed the obscurity of his family's past to worry him. He was able to have the best teachers, read the most inaccessible books, travel over several continents, ignore the passing of time.

His culture was vast and insatiable for that period, and he was able to continue nourishing himself from all existing sources as long as his vitality of spirit should last, and his fortune too of course, since merely by travelling untiringly he succeeding in finding out what was forbidden to a person with fewer resources. Nonetheless, his solitude was beginning to affect his life. He realized that, despite having travelled through so many countries of the world, discovering a great number of things in each one that gratified his curiosity and enriched his already extremely vast knowledge, nowhere had he left any friends behind. And this failure turned into an obsessive torment for his refined soul. He thought perhaps that no one wanted to have him for a friend because they all feared being reduced to simple idiots before the tremendous breadth of his culture, so evident in the simplest sentence, in the most ingenuous comment.

He decided that only by ceasing to acquire any new knowledge would he cause less of an impression and thus he would be able to gain friends. But he continued to be as lonely as always, in every country, every season of the year. Finally he resolved not to travel any more, to free himself completely from all the culture that separated him from his fellows and frustrated the possibility of his feeling himself truly attended for once. And the only thing that came to mind in order to manage an exploit of such dimensions in a minimal amount of time was to fill his mind with what were called random-choice books, innumerable books about all kinds of subjects alien to his range of interest (which in itself was exorbitant), for the purpose of producing a paralyzing saturation that would actually be quite perilous, to the extreme of being able to bring madness down on him. But he was confident, and quite justly so, that total forgetfulness would be a kind of escape, an opportune defense mechanism against the loss of reason.

After having spent years reading the best part part of the books in the Alexandrian Library he went out on the streets, and ignoring the frightful conflagration surging behind him he allowed himself to be led along by the monstruous confusion that swelled in his brain. On more than one occasion he was on the point of being knocked down by the fleeing mobs. He knew himself absorbed, out of contact with what was going on around him, but it was as if that disorder were taking place in some other man only remotely associated with his own person. He still considered himself lucid since if he were not so he couldn't have been so conscious of his obliviousness. It would not take him long to forget. Already he was uncertain of the name of the city whose empty streets he was going through.

He was unaware that, many centuries later, he was still walking past astonished eyes that watched him strolling down the broad avenues lined with illuminated display windows. With a vague smile, he returned the greetings of a man who greeted him, almost touching him. He went on greeting the other endlessly, gratefully, with the remote intuition of a friendship about to come into being at last. He didn't understand why that hand, moving tirelessly, kept being raised, but he would not be the first to lower his own hand.

Night fell on the department store window and only then did he think it prudent to abandon the greetings. His new friend must be expecting him on the other side in order to make this first meeting more companionly.

He made an initial movement with his head and immediately crashed against the glass with his whole body.

# *METAMORPHOSES*

## recollecting out of boredom

a pair of brilliant colored parrots are swaying back and forth fussing over each other. They shake their feathers and from time to time make a racket with their chattering in the hot afternoon. In the sky, heavy storm clouds begin to form threateningly and drift slowly over the cages. "Shit! Cunt! Your mother...," they scream whenever anyone draws near. And then the horrified nuns rush to hurry us away.

We are now in front of the monkeys. They watch us with their nervous little eyes. They scratch each other and hold in their little fingers the fleas they have picked off. They contemplate them with fascination and then eat them, making a peculiar sound with their teeth. Some of the monkeys are swinging by their long tails, others leap around and pirouette. We stop open-mouthed close to the heavy bars when we notice two monkeys masturbating ceremoniously without ceasing to watch us. It almost seems to me that they are smiling, and I'm on the verge of asking Mother Visitation the significance of their movements when the nuns hurriedly let us know that we cannot stay here, that we should go to see the lions.

There are three of them, of different sizes; they do not move. They look at us impassively with their yellow eyes. The muscles across their backs flutter from time to time. Last year a cub died, the caretaker tells us; he is an old man who likes to talk with all the visitors. They were able to get the other one away from the lioness in time, though she had tried to kill it as well. He explains to us that this is due to an instinct of some kind. I must not have heard him well. He was probably talking about some other lioness that attacked the cubs out of jealousy. Mothers do not kill their children. Anyone knows that. To the contrary, they take care of them, they protect them. That's why God made them, I think.

The snakes make me afraid. Enveloped in coils that apparently never end, they seem to be sleeping. Toward the back of the cage a thick, nearly black snake is dragging itself along, curving over a piece of wood in a disgusting way. It seems strange to me that they have no feet but that nonetheless they are able to move with such speed. I'll have nightmares tonight, I tell myself, and then I run toward the little enclosure where the turkeys are.

I watch their slow step, and it strikes me as comical. Their plumage is of a greenish black with a copperish glinting, and their heads are naked and rather small, covered with red fleshy growths and bearing a stiff crest on top. Some are very large. The peacock is lovely. It must know that I am admiring it because it has begun to spread its tail like an enormous fan with green feathers and hues of gold and blue. Oh yes, it is certainly proud, you can see that.

Now the nuns are beckoning to me. It's getting late, they tell me, we must be leaving. But we still had not seen the deer, with their big, melting eyes and their branching horns. And the porcupines, their bodies covered with spines. We didn't get to see the fish either. I thought that would be for another day, but they never took us back again.

The memories of certain people are like opaque mirrors; the images that gather on the surface do nothing more than muddle up the whole set. On the other hand mine are of a terrifying sharpness; they fix themselves one after the other like photographs placed in an scrapbook in the order in which they were taken. I am able to recall pleasant moments of my life, but those only come into my mind with an effort of will. There are other experiences, disagreeable ones, that are always surging in like cruel waves to erase in a moment what I wish to retain and cruelly set in place what I should like to forget . . .

And a wave came swirling toward us down low and wet our feet as you were trying to tear at my blouse. I bit you on the arm, pulled myself away, and threw myself running into the water. It was tepid, it tempted me with an unusual delight to penetrate into its mystery and to join myself with it. The further out I went, the more I felt that it was the ocean which was swimmming so rapidly toward me.

I hardly realized that I was going under now, but when I had to come to the surface for air with an abrupt movement that was more a reflex than a deliberate attempt to keep from drowning, I heard a vigorous splashing beside me. I looked around for you to ask for help because I was no longer touching bottom, but I didn't see you. Something went around my legs beneath the water, and for an instant I was afraid it was an octopus. I felt myself being dragged to the bottom and pawed over for several moments while my lungs, filling with water, were on the verge of bursting.

I awoke on the sand, spitting up water, all my clothing in shreds. You were looking me proudly because you had just saved my life. I got my breath back little by little. When I felt stronger and more clear in my mind, your opened mouth came down on mine. I became conscious of my nakedness when you squeezed my breast until it hurt. I hated having you inside me when I saw on your face the same smile the monkeys had behind their bars, when I realized the pleasure I was giving you against my will, although this time I was not only a spectator. Afterward, while you rested spread out on the sand like a giant mollusk, I let that rock come down with all my soul on your suntanned forehead. And it was I who was smiling then because of the pleasure your sudden, definitive grimace produced in me.

Immersed in the tedium of these endless mornings of such clarity that it hurts my eyes, I squeeze them tightly shut and the darkness is filled with luminous spots. I'm reminded of the blind. They don't even see spots. I look straight ahead, challenging the light. It hurts, but I resist for a few moments. I wish a little of this light would seep into me and that I could acquire the gift of transparency.

Afternoon has arrived as if sliding in; I look out the window and depart from my body, moving in an indefinite way until the moment comes when the last reflections of the sun become narrower and narrower on the horizon.

Now I have merged with the sunset and am turning into the calm, peaceful night that comes through the window from which I allow myself, completely absorbed, to be enveloped in my own tenuous darkness.

# the glasses

      Pepe screamed in fright that my face had turned into that of an owl, a mammoth owl. I supposed that in some fashion my new glasses with their thick lenses and the dark color of the heavy frames around them had made me look lke that. He didn't even recognize me when he opened the door. He became extremely pale and began to scream like some insane person until he fainted. I had never seen anyone so frightened. His reaction made me laugh at first. I didn't understand the change my glasses provoked in others' perceptions. I had to throw a glass of cold water on him to bring him to. When he finally opened his eyes, they almost popped out of their sockets when he saw me bent over his body trying to control my laughter. He begged me to run to the mirror and look at myself. I did so, though with some hesitancy because I thought he was pulling my leg.

      I couldn't believe it. Instead of my own face, I saw the enormous brown ugliness of an owl's face with its scared look. The very large and solemn eyes were each ringed by a sort of disk made of gray feathers. They looked at me flabbergasted, penetrating. I felt that they reached into the depths of my brain. Pepe found me seated before the mirror, absolutely overwhelmed, with my head, which now seemed terribly heavy, between my hands.

The more I think about it, the more I think that I was not that owl, or else that it was not I. There has to be a logical explanation, an error in perception perhaps. Maybe the lenses had gone through some sort of momentaneous distortion or they were dirty with dust from my cleaning the basement this morning. Who knows? I can't understand it. But in some way that damned owl had managed to get its reflection superimposed on mine in the mirror. The strange thing is that I am sure there wasn't any owl behind me, right in the middle of the morning and inside my own room, that might be able to project its image that way. No, it's ridiculous to try to explain it in this fashion, since Pepe was the first one who saw that enormous brown head on my shoulders. I was afraid to confess that I too was seeing the same thing in the mirror. That was when he asked me to take off the glasses.

The transformation was radical, it was miraculous. We both agreed that my face had returned to normal again. I was myself once more, the same as ever. Therefore it was the glasses that created the distortion, not only when I looked through the lenses but also when others saw me with them on.

We felt pleased, thinking we had discovered some magic spectacles. It had only been a couple of days since I had gotten gotten them from the optician, and while there I had thought them normal. I could even see much better. Since they were only for distant seeing, I hadn't put them on again until this morning.

For the fun of it, once over the shock, I put them on again. I made all sorts of clown faces in front of the mirror and the chest of drawers, and Pepe nearly died laughing. The big ugly head imitated my funny faces grotesquely, mimicked my shape and the tilt of my head, my lips in their whimsical distortions, my tongue sticking way out and drooling. Only my body kept on being the same, as if the other were simply a mask that didn't affect it. I believe that is the way we both understood it at that moment. Then something terrible happened. We had gotten tired of laughing by that time and, besides, my neck hurt and so did my mouth from so much contorting and grimacing. Pepe had stretched himself out on the bed and I was sitting on the floor, gasping. It occurred to us to wonder, and that's the way we spoke of it, that no matter how magic the glasses were, this still didn't explain how other people could see my face transformed by the simple fact of my having put them on. I could justify the distortion of what I saw through the lenses, even though it had produced only one specific image, but the rest of it still seemed puzzling. Trying to discover an expanation of the matter, I took the glasses off. Pepe recognized my usual face right away. But when I lifted my eyes toward the mirror, I only saw in it the bed in the background, with the reclining body of my friend. I stood up with one bound and glued my face to the glass. I was not reflected there. I screamed. Pepe came over to me. He asked me what the matter was. "I'm not there!" I exclaimed, pointing to the mirror. "What do you mean, you're not there?" he responded in alarm. "Are you crazy? Look at yourself there, everything is OK, you're the same Raúl as ever."

I looked again. I didn't see anything. That is, I saw everything there was in the room, including Pepe standing next to the empty space where I should have been. But my figure definitely was not reflected. Pepe insisted that yes, he saw me as clearly in the mirror as he saw himself beside me. I didn't know what to say or do. I thought I was losing my mind. Instinctively I put the glasses on again and immediately there reappeared in the mirror the owl's head joined to my body. Pepe realized that he was on the verge of witnessing a nervous collapse. He made me lie down. He took the glasses off me and went to the telephone. I assumed he would call a doctor. Afterward he went out, taking the glasses with him. I shouted to him not to leave me alone, that at least he should give them back to me so I wouldn't feel this horrible lack of reality. He didn't want to. "Rest a while and don't think of anything," he said. "I won't be long."

The blood that is gushing now from this wound is running over my hand and staining the sheet just as naturally as I had always imagined it might. For red is a festive color, common to humans and birds. One may bleed to death while grasping a branch, keeping watch over the calmness of the night with profound eyes. Or stretched out on the bed, without identity or memories, perplexed about the paradoxes of the day, hearing vaguely that someone is opening the door to the street and drawing near in order to diagnose—already too late—what is making itself quite evident.

# lake outing

The summer was already tiresomely hot during the sleepless nights, a new excuse for our not communicating with each other. But that morning I was happy because we had been invited to the lake. It had been a long time since we had gone on an outing together, almost as long as it was between Humberto's most recent kiss and the void that now was turning us into strangers. I suppose that the daily contact with his young women students must have had an influence over his distancing himself from me. He always said he was too busy with his reading and his research, but I was just bored to death, shut up in the house or walking in the park by myself.

At exactly three John and Magda came to pick us up. They made an enchanting pair. They had only been married for a year, and it was difficult for me to stop envying that halo of peace, love, and understanding which appeared to surround them every time we met at the cinema, the supermarket, or on the street. They did everything together and shared everything. Magda told me that John helps her with the household tasks, with shopping. She told me this as if it were the most natural thing in the world, without knowing that she was describing experiences very foreign to me in my relationship with Humberto. He never helped me with anything. "I work with my brain," he exclaimed every time I asked him for help. "I don't have time to waste washing dishes or going to the store with you. That's what you're for, isn't it?"

I hadn't dared to ask him again if we could go out together and try to enjoy the little things of life as we used to. But now summer was coming, and classes were finished. He couldn't invent excuses any longer. If he didn't love me, he would have to tell me so clearly. And in that case I wouldn't have any reason to go on with him. Therefore, in a certain way, the excursion to the lake would determine our future.

During the trip we talked animatedly. Humberto was terrified of gossip and so he tried to conceal our problems at all costs. Anyone who saw us laughing and singing on the way to the lake would think we were the happiest couple in the world. I'm certain that John and Magda thought so.

When we reached the lake the rest of the group were waiting for us with the meal already prepared. We spent a little while talking, telling jokes. Then someone suggested that we go in swimming. Those who brought their bathing suits went in right away, and the others remained seated, listening to the music on John's portable radio. After awhile Magda recalled that she had a ball in the trunk of the car. Everyone stood up ready to play. I looked at Humberto. His eyes told me that my presence was bothering him, that if I were to play he would no longer be able to rein in his emotions. It was the same feeling I had had so many times when he was with attractive girls he couldn't stop staring at with unmasked lust, despite my being there.

I said I had a bruised heel and I really would prefer to go on sitting at the table, watching them play. As Humberto jumped, laughed, or shouted something having to do with the game, I understood that his whole being manifested a desire for freedom that would not be put off. I was nothing but a hindrance. I came to this notion with a sharp pain, since from the beginning I had held the losing hand and our marriage was just a game played under false rules, or at least, under rules that were valid for only one of the parties.

Humberto and I had argued violently every time I mentioned the possibility of my going away forever. On those occasions he got like a little boy afterwards, begging me to stay with him. He said he loved me in his own way. I had always ended by accepting his pleas, half believing in this hardly noticeable love that he said he felt for me. I suppose that at bottom Humberto did need me, but for things more practical than tenderness and understanding. Someone had to cook for him three times a day, clean the house, do the shopping. One day I realized that it wasn't I who was exciting his senses the few times he made love to me. I merely served as a permanently available receptacle in which to place the product of a sensuality activated who knows where or by whom.

Every time Humberto jumped up to catch the ball, I felt more and more like a thing, like the table on which my elbows were resting. Perhaps if he had looked at me even once while he was playing, not tenderly but simply to know whether I still was in possession of my status as a person, things would have been different that afternoon by the lake. But Humberto spent an hour and a half involved in that game body and soul, oblivious of my existence, free of all ties, feeling himself a bachelor once more. And I didn't want for him to think that things were actually any other way when he finished the game.

I was toughening, growing harder with the contact of my elbows on the rustic picnic table where the plates, cups, and dirty napkins still remained. I had to unlive through him the time he had lost with me, that I had lost with him; I had to return every one of those hours to its beginning. The shouts and laughter were fading away. Only hazy outlines of the group remained. I could no longer place the angle from which my diminishing capacity for perception sensed the life around me. A new feeling of freedom began to settle on me despite the now nearly absolute hardening.

On finishing the game they were all greatly surprised not to see me. They looked for me everywhere for hours. Night was penetrating the thick underbrush when Humberto became absorbed in something, looking toward the lake, as if weighing a suspicion. Someone offered then to go to the city to call the police. The others sat down around me, almost without speaking, looking at me without seeing me. Humberto put his two hands on top of me and in a reproachful tone said, "She probably jumped in the lake, she's just a crazy woman."

The police arrived. On their hands and knees they covered all the same spots the group had already searched. "Everyone go back to your houses," a voice ordered. "Tomorrow we'll bring divers in to search the bottom of the lake." They told Humberto, "You too, Señor Cuellar. You'll be kept up to date on things. I'll leave an agent here in any case."

Actually, my love, since you used to be unable to appreciate me as a woman, you won't recognize me now, either, now that I am a part of the molecular structure of this table. So no time has gone by. It's starting over. I know how to be happy.

# germination

*For Anna María Acuña*

He opened his eyes slowly, fearfully. Then he could see, in the midst of the familiar old furniture flanked by the roughly curtained windows, what was causing that strange smell he had felt as a foreboding in the midst of his sleep. And in spite of the intense heat from being shut in at midday, he shivered, shaken by a mortal cold.

Before him the plant was scaling the back of that emptiness and spreading as if there were an invisible wall there or a firmly rooted shrub. The more it advanced toward his bed, that intricate shield of lianas which was eating up the space, occupying it in dimensions that were getting larger and larger, the more his eyes were becoming fettered by the sticky look of that enthralling green conqueror. Knowing he wasn't dreaming, he perceived that threatening progress with all his senses but not his understanding, and he shivered again. There was no escape route possible. When he finally understood what the result of his great dedication to botany was to be, he closed his eyes to the absurd.

The twining leaves were already embossing their greenhouse chill on his skin. His muscles were contracting. The rustling from that verdure together with the simultaneous injection of a pasty substance through his skin was overpowering him. He wanted to be able to lose himself in the secure world of sleep again, where the lack of verisimilitude had nothing to do with reality. But this never got to be more than a vague desire. A woody sort of stiffness has gradually begun to spread itself throughout his body. He feels the sap making itself heavy in his bloodstream, and also how his blood itself is beginning to harden, drop by drop. Without wishing to, he is amazed at the degree of hypersensitivity that is filling him. He knows now that his tongue has ceased to be the only vehicle of taste. What seems like tons of bitter, rustling, algid verdure are already closing off eyes, ears, nose, mouth, and erogenous zones. It is impossible for him to open his eyes, since leaves are sticking tightly to his eyelids. He would like to see the form once more, to observe its texture, its dimensions. But he guesses that his cartilaginous framework no longer exists, that the boundaries of his skin have lost their autonomy, that the process of osmosis is now well along. He tries to assay the scientific value his discovery would have had and laments that he is not filming this phenomenon. Who would have thought that carnivorous characteristics and the osmotic process could coexist in those seeds?

When his sister entered the room she turned livid. A formless thicket had germinated on the old bed, that enormous bed with its wide, baroque headboard, the bed that had belonged to their mother. The matted growth covered it completely and spilled down both sides. Immediately her attention was caught by the intense odor like eucalyptus that floated throughout the room. A new mad passion, she thought; another experiment. Oh, how long, o Lord! She would have to speak very severely to the kid this time. It's all right for him to be crazy about botany, to bury his seeds by the windows when there aren't enough flowerpots, or in little piles of damp earth right on the floor that she tries to take such good care of. She could tolerate all that from the kid. After all, they didn't even have a patio. But on Mama's bed—that's too much!

She ran to open the windows, thinking what a fool her brother was. All that knowledge about plants, and still he would expose himself to asfixiation by sleeping with them all around him. But where could he be? She hadn't seen him go out. Last night she heard him come lurching in, something unusual for him, and right after that he must have gone to sleep. Yes, she had to give him that, he didn't have any vices. At least she didn't know of any. The only thing that mattered to him was reading and experimenting with things, she thought. Some day he would be a great scientist. She smiled. The next step would be the university. She would help him pay for it. There he would have a modern laboratory, though he might have to share it with the other students. Yes, the little celebration at the end of the course was justified. He's a good boy. But, what's all this, for heaven's sake?

The smell persisted. A slight dizziness made her steady herself on a chair. What a strange plant! How was it possible it could cover the whole bed in such a short time this way? She approached curiously. It seemed to her she perceived a slight trembling in the leaves. Then, absolute calm. The odor vanished as if through a spell. It must have been the fresh air that . . . But no breeze was coming in. The morning was oppressively dry.

She observed the unusual rectangular shape more carefully. The green seemed to be intensifying, and it hurt her eyes. She didn't know anything about plants, in her ignorance they were all alike; but the curious shape of these leaves, their great number, was making an impression on her. That boy wouldn't believe that she was going to clean up his bed. The excuses he always gave wouldn't be enough this time. The minute I see him I'll tell him . . . She shut her eyes anew before the intensification of greenness. I don't understand what's happening. That shining . . . And how ungrateful he was. When Mama was dying she should have had the bed instead of giving it to him as if the back pains her narrow cot always caused her weren't important any more. But the deceased woman loved the boy so much, more than her daughter who had never demonstrated much culture. And besides, her rather brief will said clearly that the bed was to be given to him.

A rending scream pierced the waves of heat that were coming into the room and was prolonged in the distance like an echo. Without realizing it she had stepped on some leaves that had fallen to the floor, crushing them against the wood, leaves that had not been there moments previous. Now she saw, without being able to articulate her terror, that from the fragments still underneath her feet a greenish red was flowing thickly, climbing over her feet, winding around her knees, encircling her waist, kissing her breasts, stalking her open mouth from which the second scream would never escape now.

## evasions of death

i was walking along trying to keep my boredom rolled up at the bottom of the pocket in my oldest pair of pants. I had already covered several blocks with my mind totally blank. Reaching the corner I sensed that a strange, empty sensation as if from a suction cup was interfering with my legs and my desire to move any more. Here I have spent my days as if they were nights and the nights as if they didn't exist. A little while ago, just before becoming incorporated into the lamp post I casually put my hand in my pocket and demonstrated that my entire finger fit in the hole.

When I don't have anything to do, and that's always, I tell myself that I was a little boy once like everyone else, with toys and certain convictions learned at school as dogmas. I had friends and birthdays with birthday parties and the usual quota of illnesses. Surely things happened to me that others might remember with pleasure, embarrassment, or at least indifference, from their perspective as adults. I remember nothing of that. Occasionally, to make time pass, I try to poke into that past. I search for meaningful scenes, conversations, fragments of events that must have taken place. Nothing. It's as if I simply leaped over that beautiful stage which children usually go through. Perhaps I was born as an adolescent the time I was hunting sparrows in the underbrush with that old slingshot and my father beside me, urging me on. It is only after that experience that certain recollections begin to acquire any life. But I was no longer a child then. I do remember, for example, the tiny breasts on the Colombian prostitute who couldn't have been more than sixteen and who asked me not to hurt them that way because I'm still almost a little girl yet and I don't want them to get ruined. And the time the condom fell out of my billfold where I kept it and came to rest on the papers being examined by the woman behind the desk at the travel agency. The bright red color that came over my face together with the effort not to look at my father standing next to me are things one doesn't forget easily. But I have the impression, and it's not a pleasant one, that it was someone else instead of me who used to be that child, maybe without even knowing it, somewhere on this planet or another, perhaps; who knows? It is probably true that we are lived from other dimensions.

Now that I see the people going by me from this rigid evasion that signifies my having been integrated into the composition of this lamp post on any old street, I give myself the luxury of demonstrating that time is nothing more than a ghost that pushes us imperceptibly toward the return to zero with a slow infallibility that we cannot hold back.

A man is shoving a woman gently against this post; I can feel her back touching me, the joining of her buttocks, but it's no longer like it used to be; it doesn't phase me. One day you catch sight of a pair of eyes that are gazing at you, you notice a beautiful body inviting you for a little entertainment, and you even hear those words you've dreamt of so many times. So you screw, and after that experience you do everything possible to close off the avenue to love, or maybe to make way for it, whatever suits your temperament. And if anyone like myself ends up falling in love, it turns out that death takes offense and decides to visit a little early. And one day your instinct, the family doctor, or death itself disguised as weariness or the most overwhelming boredom you can imagine tells you that there's not much time left and so why go on accumulating illusions. And that's when you start wandering around without any particular destination, hands in your pockets, mind a total blank, and a predisposition to phenomena such as this one of abandoning your own physiognomy and turning yourself into an integral part of a lamp post.

If this bastard wants to spend the whole night nibbling at the woman's ears, brushing at her breasts while he goes through all sorts of arguments in order to be able to take her to a hotel, that's his problem. I will have to abide his presence until the woman gives in or he gets tired. In any case, I won't be running around on the streets again in a body that knows it's condemned.

As long as my will preserves enough energy to bring off mutations that allow me to go on escaping indefinitely, I'll continue sticking to the things that attract the least attention. Or to those that make an impression on their own merits, what difference does it make? Like these firm buttocks of the woman who is now telling this guy to go to hell and who, if I'm not mistaken, is about to move on at any moment.

Now she's leaving, taking me with her. I feel the anger in his gaze, which catches fire with my new look. I'll just have to get accustomed to the swaying beneath this light and softly provocative material.

# pigeons

*For Anna María Pujol*

time weighs heavy in this dry emptiness that presses on my stomach. The warmth of illusions still is there in the balls of my fingers. So many things could have been done. But that obsession with four walls and a roof of one's own, with a piece of land, a wire fence and several dozen hysterical hens running about in the patio, pulled them out of their right minds. To save for one's old age was more important than enjoying the daily harmony. Spontaneous gestures were missing; so were smiles. And shouts became plaited together, cases built. It succeeded in petrifying all humanity, all feeling in them. We were turning into a family of things.

Blood was running in the country and all justification remained in the volatile regions of the ideal. Lies and conjectures came tumbling after each other, one by one. Papa wanted to stop being a thing; he thought he saw imminent perils. He sent me far away and stayed behind protecting his egoism. We will join you later on, they said. His kiss followed as an obligation, so as not to break with appearances.

That afternoon I went to bid the hens goodbye, forgetting that they had been served at table a short while before. I had been so involved in my thoughts that I hadn't connected the meals with my winged friends. I finally wept on the plane which every moment carried me further from familiar landscapes and memories.

We landed at night. The clash with another culture shook me out of my torpor. I found myself obliged to react in the face of a new language and this new life organized around rules and schedules possessed of a chilling clarity. Since my arrival the promises have become a long and anguished wait. My parents' lies come better and better disguised in every letter.

Someone told me once: you are too sensitive, like a pigeon. It was a revelation. I tried to harden myself. But one day I made a visit to the park.

My eyes were full pigeons. The white, gray, and black of their feathers recreated the loneliness I bore imprisoned in my eyes. They arrived in flocks every afternoon. They perched in the trees and on the benches, always pecking about, cooing among themselves, cooing at me from a distance. At first I was afraid to approach them. I didn't want to frighten them. I assumed they would be like me; I get scared at footsteps, voices, looks that are deliberately directed at me.

I envied them. Those pigeons had no problems. Their unusual sensitivity alone made people look out for them. Every afternoon there came children with astonished eyes to throw them kernels of corn. Now I know that in reality they lack the timidity that everyone attributes to them. I know it because today I was able to touch them; they ate from my hand.

One pigeon kept looking at me a little while ago. It was trying to explain something to me. Maybe it will take some time, but I know that we'll be able to understand each other. I feel happy. This morning I was able to tear up the most recent letter without the least remorse. I am beginning to be free.

Another afternoon of sun and hopes. The air sparkled in my lungs. By the fountain I am thinking the same things I thought yesterday, but now without rancor. Everything has its sound. I hear the grass growing, I hear my hair lengthening diminutively, beneath my feet I hear the ants running around. I don't want to hurt them and so I lift both feet and sit crosslegged on the bench.

The pigeons understand each other by means of a pleasant cooing sound. It won't be long now before I understand them. There are times when everything sounds like a life already lived. But now it all exists in a new shape, a more harmonious one. Everything has its reason for being, and I feel myself a participant. Before, events took placed without my being involved. I suspect that the pigeons have contributed to the change in some way.

This is a transitory stage. The tickling sensation that ran up my arms a little while ago when the first flock got to the park told me so. I was expecting them as usual. They know now why I like them. Now I feel that my mouth wants to elongate in a strange way, and it is pleasant to feel this new stiffness that obliges my lips to extend themselves, forming toward a point. My arms too, resting at my sides, seem to want to broaden out, forming clear stratifications.

They are surrounding me. In the distance I see people passing, old men reading newspapers, children playing, but I don't distinguish them anymore. The pigeons don't gather around any other being as they do me. They have accepted my trust. Now I don't need to bring them corn any more. They don't rush away after pecking at my finger. My shoulders and head are spotted with feathers. Their softness, which they left there when they sought contact with me, remains in my hands. A light breeze which lifts their feathers comes in off the ocean. They are floating in front of me. Everywhere they are rocking back and forth, gray, white, and black blended together. Countless numbers of pigeons jump, take flight, perch, and once more take flight emitting that short, soporific sound that I know so well. Yes, I am happy. I am beginning to share in their joy. Why return to the damp room I live in when here we can look at each other for hours, understanding each other? It wouldn't surprise me if some child didn't offer me peanuts out of a paper cone one day.

I don't recall the night coming on, and yet just a while ago it was dawning already. The pigeons were watching me silently. There are more than ever this morning. They haven't tried to rest on my shoulders nor even to approach. I stretch my hand out to call them but instead of coming near they move away a little, leaving a breach in the compact presence of their feathers. They seem to have come to an agreement and now they are meditating.

I cast my eyes through the aperture and there I see a young woman walking by. She looks over here and laughs. She spills the kernels held in her hand all over the ground and with a gesture invites the pigeons to draw near. They pay no attention to her because they are watching me.

Don't reject her, I tell my friends with my thoughts; don't reject me. She is as sensitive as I am, as you are. Don't you see, she can't hold back her weeping? The gray mass dissolves in an instant and a huge number of pigeons come close. They peck here and there. One of them has lit on my head, it settles on me. Others crowd onto my shoulders and cover them completely. I don't see her now, the girl can't see me. A soft tickling sensation is caressing my ears, as well as her ears; it runs down my spine, and through hers; it goes through my arms, it goes through hers; it settles finally in the soles of our feet.

Through the branches of that tree a playful shaft from the sun succeeds in transfixing the solid wall of feathers with its warmth. Now the girl's head emerges from among the wings. She raises a hand, I raise mine. Suddenly the gray mass begins to rise. The gradual beating of the wings keeps tracing new varieties of colors. She continues waving to me from the cluster of feathers that is lifting her, and I wave at her. They are carrying me away in a tight formation, and they are taking her too.

We make an effort to see each other better. But I must seem only a colorless little dot to her as I penetrate the first cloud; I can't distinguish her any longer now that another cloud higher up is absorbing her.

# *INCIDENTS*

---

## the spectacle

*For José Manuel Bayard Lerma,
a poet from Panama.*

He slept with the blond the first night, made love with the brunette the second night, and spent the third night with the redhead with the innumerable freckles.

Later on he wanted to be with two of the girls at the same time but since all three were intimate friends and all had the same kind of affection for him, he feared to offend one of them if he invited the other two for the night, and therefore he ended up making love with all three in the wide bed he'd had installed months before, anticipating whims of such like.

Then after that, custom took over, and every night the four friends shared the same intimate pleasures. None ever had reason to complain about the others, since their satisfactions were always individual without ever ceasing to derive from activities that were essentially collective at the moment of their fullest realization.

Some time passed and at brief intervals the three women evinced unmistakeable signs of being pregnant. When it came time for them to go to the hospital to give birth, the man had to sleep alone once more. It was a sensation of unexpected relief.

Still, he dreamed again as he had not done since sharing his bed for the first time. He witnessed the difficult birth of three robust boys, the inevitable suffering of their respective mothers, and finally he saw them die. His grief was so strong when he awakened that, convinced of the authenticity of the dream when he found both sides of the bed empty, he fell into a profound lethargy.

The blond, the brunette, and the redhead came to see him all at the same time a few days later. Eager to show him the three beautiful boys he had fathered, they placed them in a row, asleep as they were, on one side of the bed and tried enthusiastically to awaken that cold body. When they became convinced of the stiffness of the corpse, they perceived for the first time the implications of the silence. They wept frantically, and the frightened babies were not long in adding their cries to those of their mothers.

The night following the burial, the three beautiful women with their sons occupied that mansion so loaded with memories. As a worthy tribute to the memory of their common lover, they initiated the rites anew. And loving each other so much, renouncing men forever, they shared their sorrows together, which the babies were unable to understand as they observed the spectacle in fascination.

## inertia

He put his face to the glass. His breath took the same shape as it always did. He never ceased to be surprised when he saw how the vapor became a spot on that windowpane. Students and workers, in a hurry as usual, were going some toward school and the others to their jobs at nearby construction sites. He vaguely recalled himself once walking along with perhaps the same haste; his gestures, his smiles before the new day had been just like those of the people passing now. He couldn't place when it was, but it was a remote past that remained suspended, a sort of limbo, in his head. And nonetheless he was always aware that time was going by and going by with it were those students and workers now in front of his eyes.

    He knew of course that time had hours that divided and subdivided themselves until you got so tired you would happily sink into total amnesia. The sequence of things that he was used to doing every day lacked the slightest importance. He hated his habit of winding up the old pendulum clock, of cleaning his shoes every day despite the fact that he never went out, of opening the door a crack always at the same time and testing the ground while looking for the bottle of milk and the sack of bread that some neighbor had continued to provide for him ever since he could remember. But a strange fear overcame him when he started forgetting everything. He was afraid of losing himself forever in a darkness where he would come to be just one more particle of dust in a corner, floating without a shred of memory nor an interval of light. As the morning splendor filters in, he keeps his eyelids shut while listening to the sounds that come in from the street, putting off the moment he ought to get up, go to the bathroom, appear at the window. And then he would remain there until noon, always seated on that rocking chair which was too small for him, until the brightness blinded him and he would retire to his room. Curled up on the yellowish mattress which was full of holes into which he would insert his fingers to pull out the fleece that he liked so much and let it sink like snowflakes to the floor scattered with books covered with mould, he would lose himself in mental meanderings until he fell asleep. Then he dreams that he is little again and that they are taking him to the museum. The huge halls bewilder him: white, shiny, deserted. Enormous pictures hang on the walls; the landscapes invite him to lose himself within them. Someone takes him by the hand. Someone very tall who impregnates the room with his tobacco smell. In another room, a vast one, they pause in front of the sculptures for a long time. The marble torsos shine as if they were sweating. There are beautiful men in athletic positions, all nude. He stretches out his arm and rests his hand on the marble sex. He awakens when a guffaw breaks out beside him.

In the afternoon he occupies the rocking chair once more and waits until the crosses formed by the bars over the window project their shadows on the floor and start to disappear. At night they don't bring him food any more, and hunger makes the hours grow longer. He used to try escaping from the anguish through those intervals of light that filled the emptiness in his head, and sometimes even this thing seemed alien to his body. A little after falling asleep, morning would arrive suddenly and he was afraid they might not have brought him his bottle of milk and his bread. He liked the rainy days in a different way. Curled up in the old rocking chair, he would watch the big drops spotting the glass and listen to the pitter-patter until he actually felt like a child for a while, and after that a fetus. Milleniums ago he used to watch his mother from this very rocking chair, so pretty and blond, drinking her tea in the afternoon. That hair would be showered with highlights when the clarity that came in through the skylight struck her on the head. In those days everything was different, ethereal.

Sometimes his mother would have friends in who would seat him on their knees and play with him until nighttime. They were lively, young, they always smelled of cologne, and they never stopped mussing up his hair until she would, distant as always, send him to bed without giving him a kiss or even a hug. He fell asleep listening to the laughter, the clinking of cups, the shattering of glasses.

It was pleasant to recall those times when they would take him to church. A hand that was plump and soft guided him, a chubby body that gave off an odor of lavender. The many candles and the smiling or patient expressions of the saints and virgins in the half-light caught his attention. The gold of those tiny flames got in his eyes with sun-like insistence, hypnotizing him. From time to time, beggars and tiny old women would light new candles after a prayer and a lot of genuflecting. And when they left he would go near the images, making the most of his grandmother's negligence, and blow on each of the candles.

The house became silent. Someone dressed in black told him that his mama had gone away. He didn't feel anything. It wasn't the first time that she had left. But there was a long box in the living room and four candles that stayed lit the whole night through. When everyone had gone to bed, he got up and on tip-toe started putting them out one by one, smiling. It was totally dark, and suddenly someone grabbed him fiercely by the shoulders and in spite of his screams locked him up in his room. He went to sleep watching paper airplanes gliding around, made out of the letters he would write while upset but not send to anyone. When he saw them turn into white butterflies, the dimensions of the room turned limitless and then he was happily taking a stroll out in the countryside.

The door to his mother's room attracted him as if it were the key to another world alien to his experiences, a remote place where there would be mysteries to discover. He was familiar with every corner in the enormous house with the exception of that room. He never had the courage to cross the threshold although he recalled having verified several times that the door was not locked as it had been before she went away.

Once his grandmother hugged him in an unexpected seizure of tenderness. Pressing his head to her beast, she told him things that at first he hadn't managed to hear because he was lost in the midst of her spongy warmth, struggling to get away from that embrace which was smothering him with so much emotion. "Try not to go out in the street so much," she was saying to him. "People are ugly and cruel out there, child. They'll say bad things about your mother." From that day forth he only saw people going past and the days repeating themselves through the window. His grandmother had left him alone, without any mirrors, with the big chairs that got dustier every day, with his paper airplanes and the window and the pendulum clock. And something was gathering within him, an indistinct idea that turned into a white butterfly trying to escape from the glass bottle that was his head. That's where all kinds of insects were gathered that had suddenly arrived and remained trapped in the emptiness of his mind.

One of his few joys had been to discover, a long time ago, that every afternoon a charming little girl would walk by in front of his window. Her steps were clumsy, but she had help from an incredibly black woman whose skin shone beneath the sun. What caught his attention was the contrast in their stature and the color of their skins. Later on, the girl, who was always accompanied, would walk with more rapid steps, pressing books against her chest. One day he noticed in surprise that her legs and hair had gotten longer. The highlights thrown by the sun upon that hair pleased him as it shook in the breeze and recalled the effect of the light upon his mother's hair when she was drinking tea with her friends.

His hands tensed over the back of the little rocking chair the first time he saw her holding onto the arm of a man. Both were laughing, and it was then that he realized that her step had turned more elastic, that her body had acquired an unusual similarity to the sculptures that were in the museum. He imagined her radiant without clothes in the middle of that immense salon. But this time as he reached out his arm he was surprised to feel the soft warmth of skin under his hand. It didn't interest him to divest the man of his clothing, for he saw him as a rigid, mutilated torso tossed in a corner, looking on impotently as he went on touching her warm body with his trembling hands. The street has already become empty when the sticky dampness that he feels on his fingers causes him to lower his head and gaze in astonishment at the limp penis in his hand.

He made up a great number of airplanes that said on them, "Look up here," and when the girl went by alone or with someone else, from behind the curtain he let them go out the window. Only once did he see her looking up and discovered with delight how clear her eyes were. After that, the airplanes went on piling up beside the rocking chair, and eventually he had a feeling that she had gone away.

One night, when all the lights in the house were lit, he decided to open the door. He had not managed to lose himself in his dreams for some time now. A constant anxiety had the insects all jumbled about in his head. The white butterfly beat its wings more furiously than ever, its immense, clear eyes trying to get out of its body. The dust made him sneeze. On the dresser made of tooled black wood he found a jewelry case. Examining it, he recalled having seen it in his mother's hands when she was putting away some things one of her friends had given her. While she was gazing at it happily, the sparkles dotted her face with diminutive bits of light, and the man's hand went down into her roomy neckline. From his own room then he had seen the man leaning over her white breast, but he didn't want to see any further and so he had carefully shut the door.

He poured out the contents over the dresser. The tarnished jewelry got his fingers dirty. At the bottom of the little case some envelopes had gotten stuck. He opened them, trying not to tear what they had inside. To see better, he ran back the heavy curtains and started sneezing again because of the dust. In his excitement he had forgotten that it was nighttime. He turned on all the lights in the room, since the light coming in through the open door was insufficient.

First he read the letters, with some difficulty. They spoke of an unusual world, one he was not familiar with. Then, as if he were going to start a game of cards, he placed on the enormous bed, one by one, the photographs which he found wrapped in a piece of paper. With unbelieving eyes he saw his mother embracing another woman, both of them naked and smiling on the bed. It seemed to him he was hearing that laughter all over again as on the nights when he used to be put to bed early. And he saw her there writhing, mocking him. The butterfly's furious beating of wings startled him. He began to run.

He opened the street door. He bumped the bottle of milk. Dawn was breaking. Fluttering away, gliding softly in the incipient reddish light, he saw a white butterfly. On the other side of the street an old woman with a black umbrella was going by.

# the schoolgirl

"It's nothing," Paula said, caressing his cheek. She had just got her eyes open at the school clinic. The nurse had gone out for a moment. "I'm just pregnant, that's all, my love!"

Alejandro swallowed hard. He was going to say something, but at that moment the nurse came in. She was bringing a glass of milk and a piece of cake. Paula sat up, trying to smile.

"It's just that I didn't have breakfast, Professor. I didn't have time. Pardon me for having bothered you. It seems I just got tired out from having run all the way from home. You know I would do anything to keep from missing class. But when you're always hurrying so much it makes you tired, doesn't it, Gloria? Especially when you're still growing."

The nurse said something the professor didn't understand. Then she asked him to leave; she would take care of the girl.

He returned to his classroom thinking how pale the schoolgirl had suddenly gotten just before she fainted while he was putting something on the blackboard. Immediately he carried her bodily to the infirmary. He still seemed to hear the rustling of voices behind his back remarking on the situation. Except that all this murmuring is not behind but before him the moment he gets back into the classroom once more. But suddenly it dies down. Thirty curious faces are fixed on his. He has the impression that they know and are accusing him. Why don't they ask him something? Isn't anyone interested in knowing how their classmate is? "Everything's all right now," he said without their having asked him anything. "It seems that it got late and she ran all the way from her house without having eaten."

They kept on looking at him. The silence had never been so absolute. Yes, they did know. They had to know. Their accusation is unanimous.

"All right, say something. Why is it so quiet? This isn't the moment to be so well behaved. Paula, I mean Miss Rodríguez, will not be long in coming back. Let's go on with the class now. I was explaining to you just now that—"

"How many months pregnant is she, Prof?" said a male voice sarcastically from the back of the room.

Alejandro felt himself grow pale. Almost immediately he felt the blood flushing through his cheeks.

"Who said that?" he asked.

All the faces kept accusing him. With their eyes they were answering him that the question had come from all thirty.

"OK, let's talk openly. You all have a suspicion. I assure you that it is a gratuitous suspicion; without basis. There are a thousand possible reasons for a fainting spell. I told you what Miss Rodríguez just explained to me. The best thing would be to wait until she returns so that she herself can—"

"Don't worry about it, Professor," exclaimed Paula from the doorway. "I can clear up any doubts."

"You don't have to explain anything to your friends if you don't want to," replied Alejandro.

"The fact is, everyone already knows anyway. I'm not ashamed to—"

"Paula—Miss Rodríguez . . . For heaven's sake, you're not going to—I mean, perhaps you shouldn't . . ."

Alejandro didn't know what to do. Everything seemed to indicate that Paula was about to confess the truth. They would throw him out of the school this very day—out of the town! The scandal would be known all over the country.

He sat down on top of the desk. The girl was beside him now, standing before her fellow students. He saw that she was determined. Alejandro recalled the afternoon she gave herself to him without the slightest hesitation, ready for the greatest sacrifices. "You're a man of experience and I can't expect you to love me in exchange for a couple of kisses," she had asserted while taking off her clothes. "If you're going to risk your job for me, let's at least make it worth your while."

"You needn't worry, Professor. You've already taken care of your responsibilities . . . Yes; why deny it? I'm pregnant!"

Paula looked at him for a moment, and he thought he would be the next one to faint.

"I have a boy friend, he's studying agronomy in the capital. Actually, we're already engaged, but it's secret. As soon as I graduate in December I'll go with him, and we'll live together until the baby is about to be born. Then we'll get married."

Alejandro breathed with relief, gratefully. Paula was very quick to make up stories, she always had been. But suddenly a doubt spurred him on. In reality he could never be sure any more.

# the mannequins

*For Verónica Zetter*

I look inside, through the window glass, and from time to time everything seems bluish. No one is there, just cardboard cartons scattered about on the floor. The suits hanging from the racks swell up as if they had already removed themselves from their supports and are beginning to glide slowly toward the door, by their own free will. On the shelves the socks and handkerchieves that have been left jumbled about quiver from time to time. A tattered curtain at the back of the shop is swaying back and forth and causing some sailboats on it to swell up to a huge size and then shrink down again, to move away and then back again, driven by the breeze coming in through the patio door.

Gazing at each other in silence from their separate corners, the two mannequins would like to shed both their inertia and the layers of fabric that had been casually draped over them for several months now. If they could take advantage of the still distant impulse of the breeze, if this should suddenly turn into a gust of wind capable of pushing them along the floor until they met each other in the center of the room, they would be able to enjoy the magic contact of their skin, now devoid of adornment, free, and predisposed to love—because then they would be a he and a she desiring each other in the solitude of a dark place.

They wouldn't suspect there might be a witness. They would gradually abandon that vertical position that has always circumscribed their being and adjust to the succesive variations of a recently discovered instinct, unaware of my presence behind the glass. I would be able to watch them stretch out on the floor, twist around among the boxes with a soft ease of plastic that has turned into spongy flesh, and couple without hestitating, just as they are doing now, because the breeze has guessed my ardor and become a wind that has matched each of my desires.

And thus, to gratify me, after enjoying our spasms we return serenely to that state of calm previous to longing, we separate and assume our habitual vertical condition once more, slide back to retrieve the fabric with the helpful assistance of the breeze, they come to a halt in their respective corners and turn rigid again, while I smile contentedly.

# the girl with the motorcycle

She hasn't seen her again. She would like to get to know her. Everyone here at the women's Y makes fun of her strong Spanish accent. She doesn't understand how they can expect you to speak impeccable English after only five months of living in this country. What would that girl say if she heard her talk? Maybe she's in the dining room with the others. It's already time for lunch. But first she will go to the lobby to call the University. Yes, that's what I'll do. If they've gotten my papers by now maybe they'll have made a decision. By good luck I did pretty well on the entrance exam for the Spanish department. Nevertheless, they make you take certain courses plus a foreign language. If she could only use English for that! What could be more foreign to her? But in any case she'll take Portuguese. That would probably be easiest because it's so much like Spanish.

She reached the lobby and saw the girl next to the telephone, engulfed as usual in a thick sweater double her size, hair all disheveled, and barefoot. She is crying. What could have happened to her? All her hair is down in her face. She has seen me and tries to hide it.

"What's the matter, Ginger?" she says in English, of course.

"They're going to let me buy the motorcycle!"

"Who? What motorcycle?"

"My parents, who else?"

"You mean you want a motorcycle and they don't object?"

"Yeah! Isn't it awful?"

"Awful! I don't understand, Ginger! Most parents would never dream of letting a young girl like you have a motorcycle! I know mine wouldn't."

"That's exactly the problem! They never object to anything. I'm free to do whatever I want. Don't you understand?"

Three weeks have gone by. Now they are good friends. Ginger has taken her for a ride several times on her enormous black motorcycle. It is a liberating sensation. The wind and the speed are stimulating challenges. It's not difficult to understand the emotion the girl feels while running at great speed against all resistance. It's a way of feeling herself alive.

Ginger wants to take her to parties but she doesn't like the atmosphere. It's another kind of challenge, but this one scares her. One time they went to a party and everyone except her spent the time smoking pot and playing children's games. A typical gringo party. They never dance together in each other's arms as in Latin America. Although there was no doubt that the music was like a restless moving of waves that brought a light shiver to her slack skin, that swept all preoccupations out of her mind. Then they all got tired and gradually went upstairs in couples. A fellow with long hair wanted her to go with him. Ginger herself was urging her to follow him.

"But why? If I don't know him . . . He doesn't even attract me," she shouted angrily.

They took her upstairs anyway. Once there, with everyone smiling, they placed a crude cigarette between her lips. Someone pinched her nostrils gently shut. She inhaled. They let go. Everything became cloudy. She ran to vomit. Behind her a burst of laughter broke out.

The following morning she woke up encircled by bodies spread around over the floor. She smelled her vomit and recalled the sudden blackout and the distant idea of a very slow fall that never reached an end. She opened the door and went out looking for some air. Ginger came back to the Y several hours later. Weeping, she asked her pardon. But she hardly remembered anything at all. But she hadn't wanted to force her. "Forgive me, honey, okay? Please, you must forgive me. I was stoned," she explained.

"I know," she said, "of course I forgive you. Just don't take me to any more of your parties."

And she didn't go to any more of them. But they continued being good friends until one day Ginger and her motorcycle disappeared. Years later she found out that she had had to be put into a psychiatric ward in Wisconsin because of the trauma brought on by an abortion she'd had. Then she felt a great sorrow, and the world took on a grayish look for a rather long time.

She often recalled that first night, when they had talked for a while in Ginger's room. In the girl's intensely blue eyes she had seen touches of green fields, leafy trees, quiet rivers where couples paddled around in primitive canoes. While telling about her excursions all over the country, the girl acquired a nearly mythic image in her eyes. When she talked about the snow that covered the peaks of the highest mountains and about how the lakes and rivers would freeze over during certain months of the year and allow ice skating without the slightest danger, she envied her friend the freedom and determination that permitted her to break with all the conventions in order to enjoy life in a healthy way. At least the stage of her life that Ginger recalled on those nights of endless talking was healthy. Then she would sing cowboy songs and protest songs gently strumming her guitar. Despite having lost a brother in Viet Nam, she seemed happy, her blond, straight hair falling down casually over her shoulders and coming to rest on her feet as she sat cross-legged on the bed. But when she raised her head to seek the eyes of her Latin American friend, the latter noticed that Ginger was crying, that sadness was actually overflowing from those eyes so large, so blue.

"Qué te pasa, Ginger? What's wrong?" she asked then in alarm. But she had to repeat the question in English because the gringo girl just looked at her without understanding.

"It's just that I ran away from home almost two years ago and they haven't even tried to find me!" she responded.

At that moment she recognized herself in her friend's loneliness. But her own came from opposite causes. She had never known freedom and now that it was facing her for the first time, she felt afraid.

# witness

She looks at me, and I know it is not me she is looking at. She spends the whole day doing it. She is crying too. She cries a great deal. Every time she finds in me the years that have gone from her, her lips tremble and with her hands she attempts uselessly to straighten out the harm done her skin by the rings under her eyes. Sometimes I hear a light moaning or I pick up the resignation of a sigh. On feeling her eyes boring into me in search of herself, I would rather not be a witness, not be the executioner, not be I. There would be others, not to doubt it, who with equal imperturbability would repay her with a distress nurtured in the sorrow of so many disappointments. But it would be others, not I, who would be making her cry.

Today she has stood in front of me thirty-three times. I'm not exaggerating. I've counted them. For hours now she's been going back and forth; she goes out on the balcony as if looking for something, comes back in again after a little while, and stops in front of me wishing for an impossible transformation. Then the tears burst out because of the impotence she sees manifesting itself in the slow decomposition of her features.

I fear for her. Never have I seen her so nervous. Everyone who has shed tears on my account, or at least because of my presence the moment a state of depression originates in thoughts of ugliness or aging, has ended badly. It is as if through time their faces were congealing on my surface, moulding themselves into images invisibly superimposed that gradually multiply their age in the eyes of those who are looking at themselves, deepening their despair to the point of some kind of climax. And afterward they make drastic decisions, or a false sense of desolation overtakes them in very little time. On the other hand, the young ones, those who in other times have confirmed the softness of their skin and the delicate firmness of their breasts with eyes that look immensely satisfied, in short, those who only consult me to assure themselves that time stays motionless in that first glance, those have never been able to leave their felicitous images impressed on me so that others contemplating themselves will assimilate them and see themselves as all the more beautiful.

Someone called her on the telephone a little while ago. Her cheeks were coloring and she could hardly manage to get her replies out. Somewhat later they came to pick her up. She had on a low-necked dress, short and brightly colored, and for the first time in months she had put on her make-up. When she set eyes on me shortly before going down they were shining with renewed enthusiasm. I felt happy for her and returned her smile.

It must have been two in the morning. I heard the front door closing sharply, footsteps running into the bedroom, and then came the peculiar sound of the bedsprings. In a moment the sobbing burst out. The room surrounding me was filled for hours with weeping: feeble, unsteady, startling.

The shadows went away, throwing light around me, and little by little my center was brightening. From the street the sounds of new activity were now coming in. I perceived suddenly that the weeping was no longer heard. I supposed that she must have gone to sleep and I wished her a refreshing dream. The blow which caused the shattering of the wasted image that had abruptly formed upon my surface put an end to that idea.

I still reflect her, thrown into the easy chair, but shattered and multiplied. The pieces of me lying scattered around on the floor pick up bits of feet, hands, breasts, tousled hair, repetitions of eyes, mouths half-open. Perhaps they are mocking her, maybe they have simply lost respect for her and are cruel in their wounding of her.

The hours will go on pressing around her skin, more rapidly than ever, wrinkling it more and more. The monotony of her gestures will be irreversible. The tenuous clarity which used to appear in her eyes on sun-drenched mornings, or when some neighbor would turn up the volume on the radio and the evocatory harmony of the music reached her, this will fade completely. She will go to sleep very early, when the afternoons begin to be tinged with shadows. And I will remain scattered about, without the company of her glances, until time finishes widening its cracks in me and I fall hopelessly from the frame.

# RE-INCIDENTS

## nereida

Every street lamp is a burning wound. The night spreads out like a nightmare from which there is no return. Beneath the mist I am contemplating you. You are here, standing, showing me—though you wish not to—the breasts that someone else is fondling beneath the persistent rain. But you are here, hemmed in by these recollections you cannot reject.

*She has stopped typing and her thoughts settle to that white Datsun where the professor is kissing her. On her lips she feels the voracious pressure of the mouth that minutes before was whispering, come to bed with me, Nereida, we cannot keep wanting each other this way every night without going beyond this. The strong hand which had been fondling her breasts through the fabric is now encircling the one that has been set free, arousing it in order to get her whole body to respond and lead it toward that surrender which the professor would like so much. She says, no, not yet, I'm not certain about myself;*

*be patient, all right? He does not insist, he withdraws his hand and permits her breast to be returned into her bra, her body to an upright position, and her breathing to its normal rhythm. Let's go now, would you mind? she exclaims while she combs her hair, and immediately they leave the deserted alley.* From a distance she senses someone speaking to her, she lifts her head and this time she hears the sentence clearly: *Señorita Moreno, don't you hear me? I'm asking you if the letter for Sr. Zuloaga the lawyer is ready yet. Yes, here it is, excuse me, I was just being absentminded, but I'll have the envelope right away.* As she types she recalls the texts she made fair copies of for her professor when he was running short of time and would bring them to class, and at the end of the hour he would rest his eyes on her and say, *can you stay a minute longer, Señorita Moreno?* All the female students would smile maliciously and pinch her before leaving them alone in the classroom. Then she would be overwhelmed by the urge to say to hell with appearances and throw herself upon him and consume him with kisses as she wanted to be doing now instead of typing this address in English that she now knows by heart from having prepared so many envelopes for her supervisor. But the professor is not near her, he's not even in the apartment on that sixth floor to which she had climbed when it was raining as it can rain only in Panama and where no one pays any attention to the visitors the neighbors have. After an endless embrace that dampens his clothing and makes him sneeze, words are nearly in the way because any talking is superfluous while he undresses her with his avid hands and she shivers in anticipation of the pleasure that she has already become acquainted with and that she now looks for twice a week as if it were the nourishment that supports her, but no, it is he who is supporting her; he lifts her bodily and walks slowly toward the bedroom while she finishes doing the envelope and tells herself, *I'm such an imbecile because he isn't even in the country,* though her memories settle him in the same places every afternoon and put him through his favorite habits. Oh, if only instead of walking toward her supervisor's office to hand over the lawyer's letter she were actually bound for the professor's apartment with his stories in her hand, thinking, *I'll tell him that the one I liked best was "In the Office." Why?* he would ask her after kissing her at length and in this way thanking her for her work. *It's just that you capture so well the emotions I will feel while you are gone. And now, young lady, the letter please; don't just stand there like a post, what's the matter with you? Nothing, Sr. Saavedra, excuse me again, I just don't feel very well, you know? Then something must be the matter with you; you may take the rest of the afternoon off if you wish. Thank you, but no, I have a lot of work ahead of me, please excuse me. Whatever you like. And yes, what she wants is to set to work, to plunge head first into this stupid world of bills and receipts and letters that always have the same address, the same servile tone. It is the only way of not thinking too much about the professor, of ignoring the fact that he is far away, doubtless caressing some other body as a part of that routine that she had managed to keep in the background during those unusual but very stimulating months, like certain drugs she had read about in a magazine. Yes, being a man when all is said and done, he would be incapable, if she knew him rightly, of putting an end to boredom any other way, for fear of the overwhelming loneliness he used to fall into after the rupture of an old habit. Therefore, Nereida gets the week's bills in order and files them carefully. If she begins immediately to prepare the sales reports of the day, putting each figure down in the ruled notebook, it is because she cannot avoid the insistence with which the professor's hands keep running lightly over her body which is steadying itself all the more against the back of the chair, and she doesn't want, she doesn't want my memory of her to be capable of making me shiver like this, of causing me such real sensations despite the distance, despite the fact that it is certainly someone else who is enjoying his eager contact somewhere in that far away country. If she could only forget, if being an efficient automaton in an office were only worth something. Nereida is typing, she types at full speed, making errors, being inconceivably clumsy, losing her breath.*

You have long ago forgotten the letter that still rends my life today. Destiny has returned you to the secret corners of Fort Amador, where the pure air and the ocean breaking against the rocks used to unleash your passion. I know that someone is kissing you and that you are repeating in your memory that it is all happening for the first time; if it were not so, you would have more vivid memories that would at least make you sigh. But in your heart you have the feeling that I am encouraging those irritable movements of his out of the nostalgia that encloses me on all sides like the fog.

He never knew if Nereida managed to develop feelings for him anywhere near as deeply traumatic and obsessive as the feelings that this furtive relationship gave rise to in his own life. She was above any domination that anxiety might exercise over his thoughts. She knew how to value the pleasure of the moment itself, to suppress the tyranny of doubt, to eliminate yearnings for the impossible. Her eyes opened up unheard of avenues for him the moment they began exchanging kisses and gentle stroking until it all opened out into the surrender that would make him descend anew toward that grateful, languid look which condensed all panting and gasping and gave meaning to the deep silence that settled over them like a third presence. They would dress and minutes later the fresh air of the night was rustling their hair through the open windows as he took her home in his car to the harsh voice of her mother, to the math homework that he himself had assigned for the following day. And that's the way it was every time, a fleeting encounter that fragmented his desire to impose a more comfortable strictness upon those meetings. He would have wanted his relationship with Nereida to have a more human structure so they would be able to survive in the daylight; he would have wanted it to come from the love that joined their bodies in those moments of cool shivering. The thanks her eyes gave him when he had gratified her, the sacrifice of an attitude which was not afraid of the consequences, should have sufficed for him. But no, he wanted more, though he never knew exactly what his unsatisfied craving consisted of.

I don't hear the bells in the distance any more. The unsettling odor of tacos being cooked over charcoal has stopped reaching me. Neither do I know if I am seated on a gloomy, yellow streetcar. Or whether anyone is spying on my memories from the distant tower of some church. It is most likely that I am stretched out on the damp grass of a park, like so many dry leaves that remain in place despite the efforts of the cool wind that has loosened them. Only those things that have to do with you manage to obtain a certain ambiguous permanence. Like the sensation of your presence as you part with all show, all sounds, without my being capable of evading myself, of evading you.

Your ghost crosses before me from all the corners of my loneliness, at all hours. When I inhale the vast silence of this alien city, a few delayed gasps like the ones you poured forth while crazed with pleasure become transparently articulated. And then the moaning you thought forever dead appears and turns into this languid motor beneath the skin, recurrent like the steady drip of a futile nostalgia.

He had saved only one black and white photograph of her, which constant handling and the years had marked with wrinkles (as she too must have been), but he had also kept alive the memories of her consecutive orgasms, which both of them would count as if they had been trying to break some sort of record. His vengeance, now that so many years have gone by, consisted of destroying that reality which he had never accepted completely and reconstructing it with words elaborated from the debris to which his relationship with Nereida had been reduced. When he was capable of initiating the first literary substitutions, the most difficult ones, he was already a man of some fifty-five years, and Nereida had already been buried for fifteen in the village cemetery. In the capital, he carried on with this urgent enterprise that would not be put off, writing day and night, believing her to have been happily married in another city and surrounded by children that in other circumstances might have been his.

I would like to insert my lucid self into the pupil of your eye and turn its gaze inward, to try to see how the seams of your impassivity are made. But it is impossible. Night has closed your eyes with impregnable double bolts. Here I am, protected by the thick netting of silence and fog, sinking into the hollow of every breath as if in a swamp. Though I might manage to escape, the road to you would be a mirage. You made it disappear with the peremptory violence of that cruel, unexpected letter. I know the puddles marking your new course contend for the tenuous weight of your feet. But they also are enlarging mysteriously as they receive the unforeseen current of my tears.

Tonight there are landscapes lying in wait, soaked wet by lost songs. Hope has fallen from my hands, like a faceless child once did, having been pitilessly expelled from your womb. The wind that is now trying to scatter those fragments has been infected by this crushing sterility.

At one stroke you have deprived me of the world that I had gradually been building for the two of us out of the black fibers of your hair, day by day, through my tenacious will toward fulfillment. I recall my surprise the afternoon you arrived with a smile on your face like someone who is throwing down a challenge, with just your cool breasts under your light sweater. Just like your letter, there was nothing rash in that act, it was only to be expected; one cannot enclose what yearns to be free.

*Your recommendations are unnecessary, since I have reached a decision: I do not love you. If it had been any other way I would have given you a reply much before this . . . I love another man; I love him, I need him . . . We will be married very soon. At least that is what we have planned. It all depends on him . . . If one day I ever said or thought that I loved you, I was mistaken. Now that I know what love is, I can understand . . . I have left instructions that any letter of yours they receive at the apartment should be thrown out . . . I don't ever want to see you again . . . You never managed to fill that great empty place there was in my life . . .*

Once that obsessive labor of years was completed, with weariness weighing on him like a child that is too heavy, as much because of the dimensions of his novel effort as through a badly corroded familiarity, he realized in effect that Nereida had been reborn, reconfigured in the words upon words that he had shaped on countless sheets of paper, bestowing on her a sordid, everyday reality that she never had.

Only then, after a minute but cold reading and the most personal of satisfactions, did he understand that, contrary to the enthusiasm that had impelled him to write, he was no longer interested in bringing it to light, since his labor had only been conceived as addressed to himself. For the first time in a long while, he succeeded in putting aside all feeling of austerity and, renouncing the discipline he had imposed on himself, he smiled happily.

Without the least haste he rolled up his sleeves, breathed a long sigh, and one by one, with infinite patience and care, he started reducing those pages to the kilo and a half of confetti for which he was given a couple of coins during the last carnival days in his lifetime. He spent them on a cup of café con leche and decided that now he could die calmly; he would go back to the town from which (they discovered this one rainy afternoon by accident in a hotel bed) they had both come.

*Doubtless it is raining on Fort Amador where you surrender your kisses with spontaneous yearning. Tomorrow it will be hot, and you won't feel sorry. Here the sun will never come out because the fog together with my grief will create a single thick cloak over the city. That won't prevent your photograph, nonetheless, from giving off a vague fragrance of violets that will force me to go out into the streets to be able to breathe. By that time, as now, night will have come down like a harsh nightmare from which there is no return. The just reward earned for me by my deepest devotion.*

Due to the absolute scarcity of plots available in the cemetery at the time, the villagers who knew of his passion for Nereida thought it was a good idea to bury him just above her remains. He suspected as much when he perceived the broken sound of his own name nearby, though it was impossible to recognize her voice. It became a certainty when the first of many bursts of coarse laughter screwed its way into his ears just like another worm.

## the trunk

Lightning breaks out with a luminous jolt against the cloaked sky, and the thunder is not long in filling the room like the amplified cracking of a muleteer's whip as he hastens down the slope in order to reach the town. The house is empty except for the intense fragrance of rain and damp earth that impregnates every corner.

The wooden floor spotted with thick clay reminds me that someone was here a little while ago. At least I recall something like fleeting shadows that draw together again forming an upright figure that moves slowly toward the kitchen, disappears, then stands in front of me without having seen me. Only with difficulty would he be able to sense my diminutive presence next his feet, although I of course observe how he stoops down over the trunk that had previously caught my attention and opens it. From the pocket of his sheepskin jacket he removes a little red package and a knife and deposits them inside the trunk with obvious tenderness. He locks it with a key and now stands up. He looks at the dog-eared photograph he encountered when he put his hand into his pocket once more. From my new position on this chair I try to recognize the image. I can't because he puts it away immediately and starts toward the door. He goes out.

Outside, the sky has tumbled its blackness over the remnants of the afternoon while the rain continues falling in sheets. The wind whips the door back and forth from time to time, forcing a sharp sound from it as it bangs against the wall.

I see a shadow there. With a leap it has placed itself next to the old chair. Its bulging eyes have seen me. It jumps again. Two more and it will be upon me, and me with this hurt in my side that deprives me of my agility. Once again, and now it is underneath the table. Its throat inflates. It opens its mouth and quickly launches its sticky tongue out but it doesn't get me because I am lucky and fall to the side, too close to it. It whirls its rough, solid body toward where I am and measures the distance. Its body exudes a dampness now that envelops me. A weak chirp comes out of me that focusses the attention of its enormous eyes beneath eyelids even larger. The moment its tongue is to fall on me, I make a painful effort, jump high, and come down on top of the trunk. Immediately I discover the hole that is going to save me.

The darkness is total. The rain cannot be heard any longer. Here within, one feels a welcoming warmth that invites repose. I will have to remain indefinitely, since how will I know if my enemy has departed, weary of waiting. I can see better now, walking around among papers and pieces of clothing. I'm on top of what seems to be the package just placed here a little while back. It had a rectangular form then but now it lacks a compact texture. I rub at it and this porous surface is already getting soft. Now it tears. My antennae probe at the contents, eager to discover why this soft, nearly elastic thing wobbles so beneath my feet. At first, because of what still remains of its shape, I think it is simply a mango that is beginning to go soft. But the sticky substance that adheres to my sides is very different from the sweet sap of the fruit. I begin to suspect that this is a piece of flesh, a kind of food that I detest.

# her name is lucía

Yesterday a little girl came to see me. She said, my mother needs to talk with you. Surprised, I asked her, who is your mother, and what does she want? The girl looked at me with her big black eyes, not daring to speak. There was something in her look that frightened me. It was something like a reproach, an accusation regarding something I didn't understand. I insisted that she tell me her mother's name. Her name is Lucía, she said simply. The reason for her mission was what was difficult for her to put into words. I can assure you that I am not acquainted with any Lucía and doubtless there is some mistake, little girl. She was unable to tell me her surname. Really, you must be looking for someone else.

I was already set to shut the door when the girl exclaimed, "Aren't you my father?"

I swallowed strongly. I felt confused, uncertain.

"I think you are committing a serious mistake," I replied. "I don't have any children. I'm not even married."

"My Mama says she isn't either."
"But . . ."
"And so you can come without being afraid," she went on, with an assurance that the timbre of her bell-like voice reaffirmed.

Standing in front of this living accusation, I sought some familiar sign in her, a clue that would lead my memories to the image of her mother. In reality it could have happened with any of them, and there were so many. I didn't recall any Lucía, but then most of the other names didn't come to mind either. The situations where I hadn't taken precautions were very few, but who knows? Maybe one of those times . . .

"Mama knew you wouldn't believe me," the little girl exclaimed, showing her impatience in the uneven tone of her voice. "You are Señor Beitía, aren't you?"

"Yes, but—"

"Then here, take this."

Before I could add that there might be several persons in this town with the same last name, she had put into my hand a small cross with five tiny diamonds. I had seen that cross before, I was sure of it, but where? It certainly wasn't mine. And I didn't recall having given it to any woman.

I tried to penetrate into the world of associations and fantasies often hidden behind the eyes of kids of that age, and I asked some leading questions. I found nothing. She kept looking at me with that muffled reproachfulness that I had intuited from the first. It could be a trick. Some of the women I have been acquainted with, or perhaps someone who didn't know me at all, might well have fabricated this thing in order to compromise me. They would just need to know a little about my irresponsible past, that unrestrained life that had never had anything secretive about it. I scrutinized this thin body, her dark skin, her straight, black hair. At least she didn't look anything like me.

"What does this cross have to do with me?"

"She gave it to you one night when it was raining and there was so much thunder and lightning."

"It rains every night here, you know that."

She lowered her head.

"What's your name?"

"Lucía."

"All right, Lucía, take me to your mother."

She took my arm and led me for a long time over cobbled streets. I saw only children here and there, a lot of them, both white and brown, just Lucía's age, playing strange games. They all raised their eyes to watch us pass. That's what it seemed like to me then. Now I know that they were looking only at me. It was as if all the adults of the town had agreed to disappear at the same time.

The afternoon was dying away behind the mountains, and I was aware that we were getting farther and farther away from the village. Lucía seemed to guess my hesitancy because she exclaimed at once, "Just a little bit more. It's in the outskirts."

"What's your mother like?"

"Well, the truth is, I don't know now. She says that when you knew her all the men used to chase after her. She tried to keep herself hidden all day long so they wouldn't do her wrong. What's that mean, Papa, "do her wrong?"

"I don't agree that I am your father, Lucía. I'll be able to know more when I see your mother."

I could hardly distinguish her face now, but I could have sworn that she was struggling to keep her smile from turning into tears.

We reached there as night was falling. There were no houses about. I was going to ask the little girl where her mother lived but again she guessed my thought.

"Down there," she said, pointing to the dark, level area below us. "There's a path right here. Come, give me your hand. I know it by heart. Every day I climb up and down all the time doing errands for her. Do you know, I have been looking for you for a week, going house to house? She insisted that you still lived in the village even after all this time." Her tone of voice brightened up once more.

Prey to a guilt-ridden stupor, I recognized the shadows of the cemetery as we kept going down.

# baptism in absentia

> And I will not leave; and I'll be alone, without a home, no green tree, no white well, no blue and placid sky . . . And the birds will keep on singing.
> —Juan Ramón Jiménez, *The Definitive Journey*

Properly considered, it was not a simple premonition. What was about to happen swept my spirit down paths quite opposed to those I had always imagined for similar circumstances. But I was so convinced at that moment that everything seemed quite natural, or at least, inevitably programmed.

The previous night I had seen a face that wasn't mine at the bottom of a glass of water. I didn't recognize that scowling face. It kept on looking at me obstinately. I kept my gaze on the bottom as if it were at the end of a narrow well-shaft with crystal walls, because those sinister eyes seemed to want me to squeeze myself down as small as

I could in order to fling myself in there. I no longer resisted the force of the call. I was on the verge of losing my identity completely. What did get entirely away from me was any notion of time. Someone pulled the door open behind me and only then did I see my own face reflected in the water.

An embassy official was accompanying me. He was the one who made all the transportation arrangements, coordinated the expenses with the insurance company, notified my home. I had met him the afternoon I came to his office, assuming he was actually the consul, for him to notarize some academic papers. He turned out to to be the first secretary, a very cordial and pleasant person, the father of three wild boys whom I got acquainted with the night I had dinner at his home. To the sound of *tamboritos* and *mejoranas*, eating seviche, we called up memories of things back home.

I had wanted simply to get on the plane, leaf through a newspaper, sleep a little. As I used to do every year, going back for Christmas. Logically, this trip turned out to be the least tiring of all those I ever took. But I sensed that they must already have heard the news in Panama, which made me imagine the Tocumen airport filled with friends and acquaintances, and this caused me a certain amount of distress. I didn't dare to assume that Paula would be able to come to meet me.

On the way home from the airport there were few voices, little talk. I don't know who lifted me down from the plane. I assume there must have been the same heat as usual. Suddenly, sobbing broke out. "My son!" screamed my mother. I wanted to let her know at least that I heard her, the most important thing is that I've come back, Mama, my remains will always be close to you, think how it could have turned out differently, without their being able to bring me back, please don't cry so. The weeping became fainter and I realized they were carrying me away from her. Or else they were taking her away from me. Father, who was stronger, must have been at her side, silently, squeezing her arm. Perhaps at that moment he was thinking, as I was, about the time when a little packet of condoms had fallen out of my wallet and immediately landed on the desk of the U.S. consul, a woman with a horsy face and the stupidest questions on that rainy afternoon of my adolescence. Poor father! He didn't know where to hide. Neither did I. To get out of the situation it occurred to me to say they were just chocolates, and I even asked, "Would you like one?" The consul got embarrassed and without raising her eyes said, "Please come back Thursday for your visa."

"Poor fellow, so young, with such a future ahead of him, to die so suddenly, so far away from his country, when things had been going so well for him," Ramírez was saying. That night at his house, how far we had been from realizing that he was to see me only one more time before he would have to buy a coffin for me. "But just look how he died," commented another voice. "What was he doing in a place like that?" "Just what anyone does in a brothel when he's feeling lonely," the official justified. "I met him personally once; we heard him play the piano at home, he could have been a great concert pianist." "It appears they have already arrested that guy, the one that was the woman's lover," another person observed. "The newspapers had a lot of fun playing up the whole affair; there were even pictures." "Yes, that was a pity," Ramírez said. Afterward the voices became all mingled together, but I think he no longer wanted to talk now. The other passengers, unaware of my presence on board, must have been making an effort to accept the relative comfort of the trip, though conscious of the risk that any airplane flight implies. I was thinking, on the other hand, that death only really begins its surveillance when it is close to being realized, for it has known since the beginning of time the exact moment and circumstances of each encounter with its victims.

When that door was pulled open so suddenly, I knew by the woman's scream that my time had come. Before me I had a raging face. He was looking at me with those sinister eyes which I immediately recognized. The steel penetrated my breast, the screams grew louder behind me, and my destiny rapidly forsook the point of the knife to spread throughout my whole body and confirm my premonition. Nevertheless I was able to see the man strike the still-naked woman on the bed and then leap through the window. There was only a slight interval of absolute emptiness between the pain and the perception of the moaning. A lapse which could have lasted for a fraction of a second or an eternity, but one which signified something like a baptism in absentia.

Now, with a little luck, perhaps I may be a memory in someone's sorrow.

# NEW DUPLICATIONS

## i'm in love with you, sylvia

*For Carlos Illescas*

I watched her secretly every night. Her slim figure would begin the series of routine movements that would gradually leave her without any clothing on. Then, naked, she went into the bathroom. There the spectacle was interrupted. The window was high up and there was no way to follow the pleased reactions which the warm water surely must have produced nor the soapings over the various parts of her body nor the expressions that bloomed on that deliciously young face so fully capable of being moved. But my imagination knew how to fill in the details very well. It was only a question of wanting to.

And night after night I did want to, when I went to bed alone with my secret. First came the visual pleasures which little by little were aroused by contact with the hand that I imagined someone elses's.

Afterward came the dreams. One after the other. Almost as though they had been ordered. Always exciting. But one night my neighbor came to realize she was being dreamed into situations quite contrary to her taste. Her eyes were like arrows searching for the brain that was causing her to take pleasure in forbidden relationships. If the dream had not broken through its quivering mantle in time, perhaps by now the newspapers would be playing up a tragic event.

After that night I was afraid to go on observing her. I knew that the dreams would come again some other time. A kiss, a caress that would put the girl off, these might turn out to be too dangerous. It wasn't worth while taking that kind of risk. There were other ways, there had to be. That very afternoon I would be waiting for her. Since we hadn't ever met each other formally it was a question of tactics. The strategy to follow organized itself gradually in my mind until it got to be a precise plan.

I saw her coming. I swallowed hard and thrust any last shred of timidness deep inside me, and out of my fears I created simple phrases to use as a hook. I told her that I had a great deal of interest in talking to her in order to explain a project with great possibilities that I was putting together. An Italian consortium that wanted to film pictures in Panama using local actors. But I'm not an actress, not at all, Sylvia replied without hesitating. I'm not even interested in being one. I wouldn't have the time. Besides, my boy friend wouldn't let me.

Maybe her boy friend would change his mind, in case he actually refused to let her act in the film—something we really don't know—if he could also have a part in the picture. Imagine. Both of them would be acting together, wouldn't that be an exciting idea? A marvelous experience, something that would always bring them together facing the world, think about it. At least allow me to explain the situation a little more, I begged in my most engaging manner, placing my sweaty hand on the girl's arm. A rapid glance at her watch, a light smile, and a yes, all right, I'll listen, whispered with that soft voice which I had wanted so many times to hear—all these preceded the brief stroll to a nearby restaurant.

She walked along as if floating on air and began to lose her resistance. When we got there, she had no arguments to offer. Then I looked into her eyes. When the silence got too heavy I took her hands in mine and said simply, "I'm in love with you, Sylvia."

Her much desired mouth opened incredulously. I saw her extremely white hands, which were now loose, grow taut. I understood that her words had gotten choked off half way up and I wanted to help her. It's natural for you to be surprised, I pointed out. I know you have only seen me a couple of times near your apartment. Besides, this isn't the kind of thing you expect to hear from a stranger. Please forgive me for having brought you here to hear this. I couldn't stand it any longer. Believe me, Sylvia. I've been in love with you for several months. I dream about you. I had hardly finished speaking when I noticed how large her eyes were getting. Her long eyelashes seemed artificial but they weren't. Everything about her was authentic. I knew that only too well. I was waiting for what I already guessed at.

I confess you puzzle me, the girl began slowly. I don't know what explanation to give you for what I'm going to tell you, but I swear it's true. At night I haven't been able to sleep very well, I still can't. I feel that some occult force is moving me and pushing me around however it wants to while I sleep. For months I haven't been able to dream. Once when we ran into each other near my apartment, I felt a strange sensation pressing within my breast. The truth is that when you stopped me just now I was a little afraid to talk to you.

Are you still afraid of me, Sylvia? I asked, lightly caressing the palm of that cold hand which rested inert upon the table. I knew that you would reject my dreams since you weren't acquainted with me at all, and I have tried not to dream about you any more. What do you see in my eyes? I don't see anything, nothing at all, the girl exclaimed nervously, and then added immediately: No, that's not it, I see myself. But I don't even know what your name is. My name is Edith, Sylvia, I whispered, deepening the intensity of my gaze. We're going to be good friends from now on, very good friends. The girl did not respond.

I got to my feet without haste. Silvia imitated me. We walked together to her apartment. Without a word we went up together. Arriving at the door I was content to observe that my beloved's hand was trembling slightly as she put the key in. Let me help you, my love, I said. And we went in.

# they don't think I had a good motive

It would have happened sooner or later. At times I dared to imagine a slow vengeance, carefully calculated. But it wasn't so. And then when the moment came I didn't feel anything, not even relief.

"What will you do when you finish at the university?" a voice burst out behind me. "Do you know you've been looking at the water for more than five minutes?"

I turned and saw you close by, tall and fleshy, hair combed and much blonder than two years ago, hands in your pockets. I recognized that odd expression that never managed to turn into a smile. Or perhaps it was only the shadows playing around those pale lips I hated so.

"I'm not sure yet," I said. I was suddenly conscious of how stupid I must have appeared absentmindedly contemplating how lost in its memories the ocean seemed. It would never have occurred to you that I might be searching in the water for those nocturnal outings beside you when the future seemed so happy and certain.

"I would like to do graduate studies, and maybe teach."

I looked away. You must have smiled in your mocking fashion. The vast sorcery of the night was swallowing up my vision until it filled me with darkness. What in hell was I doing there, with you?

"Don't you think it would be a good thing to consider my offer? You're twenty-five... As I told you a while ago, I realize I didn't treat you well before and I'm ready to make amends for all that. I'm not under my father's influence any more; now I make my own decisions. I need you, Carmen. Give me another chance. You won't regret it."

I couldn't evade the fact that a few hours ago I had been filled with a great satisfaction. Papa Woodward had died of a heart attack, you told me. The owner of an extensive chain of super markets throughout several states, he had sowed ambition in you. You spoke of his death with all due sorrow, but you couldn't hide your enthusiasm. Again and again you insisted that you would manage by yourself to carve out that destiny that previously came to you ready made. And at every mention of how free we would be without him, something within me screamed out, "Finally! But it's too late. And there's still the baby!"

"Look, just because you've gone to the university doesn't mean..."

It was getting so dark I couldn't make out your features any longer. You came closer.

"You'll stay here?"

You were just humoring me. You aren't one to change your mind very quickly nor let yourself be convinced. But nonetheless it was strange how sometimes you could appear almost timid. All afernoon you had been surprising me with your calm, low voice, that unfamiliar attitude of moderation, your capacity for supplication. But two years had gone by and you would have been a fool to let yourself be swept away by your usual manner if you wanted to conquer me again.

"I never intended to leave. My place is here when I can't be in my own country. The climate is so similar, the ocean, the Spanish you hear being spoken everywhere... Let's go back."

"Now? I thought you liked this. What if we took a walk along the beach for a while, like the old days?"

"Those days never existed. I was stupid to let you bring me here. Let's go back."

You took another step and we were nearly touching.

"Carmen," you whispered, touching my hair, "you know there's no future for you alone here in this city."

"I'm going to go to school . . . and there are jobs . . . and men . . . Besides, the future is where you find yourself."

"I guess you have a right to be angry. You know, you've changed. You aren't submissive any more. And you're prettier, more mature."

Your eyes were shining as they rested shamelessly on my breast.

"I admit I didn't know how to appreciate you the way I should have before. I was worried about pleasing my father, taking care of his business. But now I give orders to the others. We can spend more time together, do sports . . . I'll take better care of you."

I felt your fingers sinking into the curve of my waist. Your warm breath was above me. Some fascinating detail about my neck held your eyes.

"I can hardly believe I've found you again . . ."

I occasionally used to model sportsware for commercial houses. One night I saw your head appear unexpectedly beside the long wooden platform where I showing a bikini, to applause. Your hand lifted to greet me. Your lips implored my attention, moving silently to say, apparently, "I need to speak to you," or something like it. I don't know if I betrayed any reaction, but I felt the tendons hardening within my breast in a strange mixture of repulsion, anger, fear. On finishing the show I escaped through the back door just in case you were waiting for me at the main entrance. Afterward you confessed that you had stayed there waiting to see me until late at night.

In those days I discovered growing within me a captivating but uncertain longing to do something to you, to hurt you, on behalf of the child you had never bothered about. It was a feeling that terrified me because of my bewilderment, and it often ended in nightmares. Like being trapped in a gigantic, invisible net which was wrapping itself tighter and tighter around me and suffocating me.

Once I dreamed about you with such striking intensity that you yourself felt frightened. I was telling you that you were being dreamed by me. You became aware of being the only person in an empty world reduced to the whim of another dimension outside your control, and this certainty bubbled hotly in your brain until your fear went beyond the limits of your mind, causing the veins on your temples to expand and get so blue I thought they would burst. And I was trembling while still asleep, in a muddled way afraid of the impact, since it was I who was dreaming about you. It was then that your eyes sought me out desperately in all the corners of the room into which the immense hollow space of the dream had turned. I heard you begging me with a frantic quivering of froth at your mouth, an insane blinking of your eyes, and a furious spinning around, begging me to leave you alone, begging me not to do that. And while dreaming I felt dizzy. When you finally managed to stand up straight you saw me before you, seated on a bed, wrapped in a blood-colored tunic that was transparent. Without moving I smiled to see you going down on your knees, placing your hands on the dirty floor, until you were on all fours in front of my knees. You kissed my feet, licked my hands, and made odd guttural sounds that appeared to be ripped out of the deepest part of your throat . . .

"Let's begin again . . . Come on, Carmen, put your arms around me!" I heard you saying now.

"No, no!" I shouted. "It would never work out. You haven't changed. You'll never change. And besides, I hate you . . . Take me back to town."

A surge of vivid frustrations filled me, setting themselves up in opposition to the humiliating arousal that ran through my back at that moment. For a fraction of a second I was afraid of weakening again, but immediately I knew I would never forgive those two years of loneliness nor your absolute unconcern about the boy. Not even a post card asking if he was well.

You tried to kiss me, and as I resisted with all my strength I saw myself painfully pushing against you in that room in the Hotel Ponce de León two years before, the morning I went in to clean thinking no one was there. The reflection of a man in pajama pants without a top appeared suddenly in the mirror over the chest of drawers while I was dusting it, and I turned around, suppressing a scream and blushing fiercely. You just stood there smiling, examining me from head to foot, a towel hanging from your hand.

"Excuse me, sir . . . I didn't want to . . . What I mean is . . . I didn't know there was anyone in here," I finally managed to say.

"Don't worry about it, love. You're not bothering me. Go on with your work, don't be ashamed."

You came nearer. I made an effort to put aside my confusion, but the words wouldn't come out. I had never seen a man in pajamas looking at me that way before.

"I didn't know the employees here were so pretty!" you murmured, brushing my cheek with your index finger. I trembled and turned red, backed away from you, and started toward the door, shouting, "No, you're not allowed to . . . ! I'll come back later."

In an instant you had placed yourself in the doorway and held me tightly with one arm while with the other you covered my mouth. Your foot kept me from opening the door. But I was able to turn my face aside when you tried to kiss me.

"What isn't allowed?" you were laughing. "That pretty girls go cleaning rooms while the guests watch them in admiration? Sure you can make an exception with me, can't you, love? I won't tell anyone."

You unintentionally relaxed the position of your foot and I opened the door with a shove.

"You are . . . wearing pajamas!" I exclaimed and went out.

You pretended to abandon your attempt and moved aside. I cursed the fact that I felt myself sufficiently alone to accept you then without knowing you well. I thought, as so many times before, that it was only in a moment of weakness that I had wanted to marry you, and like an avalanche all the countless infidelities, humiliations in front of friends, lies, insults, beatings swept into my mind. Maybe that was the moment my hatred built up so strongly. But only after you raped me on the beach did I decide to take revenge.

On the way back to town, in your luxurious sports car, you asked me once more to live with you. You didn't mention anything about our getting married again, which suited my plans. You tried to give me the impression that, as you still considered me your wife, there was no need to go through any legal processes again. I told myself that this way it would be much better, easier. Still, I neither accepted nor rejected your offer during that steady journey to your hotel, where you insisted we would have dinner together. You interpreted my silence as a tacit acceptance of both whims.

A little before getting there you mentioned Papa Woodward

again. You spoke about him with a certain vague admiration that you tried to disguise as a feeling of independence. The anxieties I had been feeling since I had, without knowing why, agreed to come along despite not having heard from you for two years had turned into restrained fury on the beach. And when I heard you mention your father again all the old vile things, which you had had an active part in, came rushing into my mind, and I trembled with pleasure anticipating the hell I would make of your life.

Papa Woodward was always a cruel, remorseless man. From the first he did everything possible to get me away from his son. I will never forget the morning he called me into his office in Madison, Wisconsin. We were living there after we had gotten married without the old man knowing anything about it. You had convinced me in some way that it was better for your father to believe that we were merely living together.

"I'm pleased you have decided to come. There is something important we must discuss. Sit down, Carmen."

I sat in front of his desk trying to feign the greatest calm. It wasn't easy for me to imitate the cold, petulant tone in which he was speaking to me. I had only seen him on two occasions before this. When he discovered that you and I actually were married he refused to visit us. I myself had informed him of the truth when I got tired of playing the role of just another of his son's girl friends.

"I must confess that I am surprised. I had the impression that we were not on speaking terms."

"We weren't, dear."

"What can I do for you?"

"I know you don't think well of me, Carmen," he said, lighting his pipe with the utmost calm. "I'm certain you know the feeling is mutual."

Behind the broad desk loaded down with papers that hid the enormity of his great belly, he looked at me fixedly, with a cold, liquid expression in his eyes. I suppose he was trying to understand the attraction you had felt for me, the one that had made you dizzy and "distorted all feeling for social values," as I found out the old man had told you once. Now he was searching in my figure, I didn't doubt it, for that mysterious something that had impelled you to get married to a hotel chambermaid with copper-colored skin. She's not pregnant—

it had already been more than a year— she's never been pregnant by him, so that can't be her motive, he must have been thinking. I think I enjoyed the shadow of uncertainty I saw there for a moment in his hard face.

"What do you want?"

"You didn't have a penny before meeting him, right?"

I felt the beating in my breast accelerating, my hands were tensing over the arms of the chair.

"I understand you were a hotel chambermaid. Am I correct? Don't hesitate to correct me if I am mistaken. Could be I'm getting you mixed up with one or another of his pick-ups. You know, at my age anyone can get people mixed up. Sit down, dear, please. Be patient a little longer. I'm not finished yet."

"Why should I listen to you insult me? Why do you hate me, Mr. Woodward?"

"Because you are David's wife," he said brusquely. "I built this corporation out of nothing with my own hands and my mind and my unyielding effort, and by God my son is going to manage all this some day."

"No one is denying your efforts. Of course, David can . . ."

"He will not be able to with you at his side. He committed a serious mistake, letting himself be seduced so, a mistake for which I will not pardon him. He cannot care for you and this business at the same time . . . And of course," he added, looking at me viciously, "there is always the obvious fact that you are not a white woman."

I stood up ready to leave. I would not allow him to break my spirit.

"Wait," he ordered. "I have a check for you."

He held it out to me. It was for a thousand dollars.

"The first payment," he said. "I've arranged everything for a quick, simple divorce. My lawyer will see you about the details, there aren't many. This is only the first of ten monthly payments that you will receive. That seems a rather decent arrangement if we consider all the factors."

"I don't want to divorce David!" I was able to say at last. "You can't buy me, Mr. Woodward! I'm not one of your maids! I'll tell David . . ."

"David has already consented to the divorce."

"I don't . . . I can't believe it!"

"He finally saw all the advantages. Plus, he asked me to explain everything to you. Since you hardly ever see each other now . . ."

"David will never agree to any such thing without consulting me," I lied, vaguely conscious of the little pieces of paper that used to be the check but now were trailing from my hand and scattering on top of the desk.

Papa Woodward asked me if I wanted to call him so that he himself would confirm it. I said yes, desperately, in case the old man had made it all up before talking to me. He placed his huge, freckled hand on the receiver.

"Do you think you're happy with him? That you make him happy?"

"Yes."

"Yes, what? the first or the second?"

"Yes to both," I responded defiantly.

"Neither," he said, sure of himself. "You haven't slept together for months. I don't even think he sleeps at home any more."

I hadn't the courage to look at him. I was devastated. While he was dialing the number of your office, Papa Woodward's face couldn't hide a smile over the triumph that was filling him. My heavy head fell. I wanted to believe that when you heard my voice you would retract it if perhaps you really had agreed to the divorce. Your father was telling you now that I was here and wanted to ask you something. The receiver swung toward me, possessed of a weighty inactivity, dangling from the cord that that hand was holding now between two fingers as if it were a toy. I had hardly begun to talk to you when you interrupted me.

"He told you the truth, Carmen. I want the divorce. As soon as possible."

Papa Woodward's features appeared to be moving absurdly over the oval face which was trading places back and forth with the desk lamp.

"Try to understand, Carmen. I'll be traveling over the country most of the time now, and I think it will be better for you to have your freedom. I'm sure you will meet other men that . . . Or maybe you'll want to travel a little yourself. You haven't seen your family in a long time . . . In any case, I've thought about it a lot, and . . ."

I found myself in the elevator crammed with people bearing surprised looks on their faces. It dragged interminably on the way down. For a very long moment I thought I wouldn't be able any more to get out of that hermetic enclosure where hot skins were rubbing against me and mocking eyes were smiling at my shame. I succeeded in making myself feel very small, as small as Jonah in the belly of the giant fish. When I got home I cried for hours. I decided that I shouldn't be part of a situation that wasn't even a cohabitation any more, since one of the parties didn't want to be there and the other was falling mortally apart.

I am certain Papa Woodward was unaware that I was pregnant the morning he spoke to me in his office, David. You were incapable of creating a new problem for yourself by telling him so. But you knew, you did know . . .

The following morning I signed whatever papers the lawyer put in front of me. I never ceased to be amazed at the lack of legal tangles and paperwork which I had assumed were normally entailed in a divorce. The judge presiding over the court I recognized as the man in the grayish beard hurriedly leaving Papa Woodward's office as I was going in. I knew that once this affair was officially over, everyone would pretend this marriage had never existed. Had it?

\* \* \* \* \*

I don't understand what is happening very well. It's as if they were trying to make me lose my mind, trying to make me believe I have already lost it. They want to get me all mixed up so I will think I am two different people: the one I know who has lived through everything that went before and the one I know who is locked up here. The girl whose experiences I am telling about is supposed to be only a fragment of the imagination of the poor crazy kid who did what she did without any explanation for it. But I know I am one single person. Even though sometimes the doubts come in, in my heart I know I am telling the truth. All the lies in the world will not succeed in making me less certain what I did and why I did it. They don't think I had a good motive. I know the opposite. You know it too, David. Your eyes betrayed you for a fraction of a second that night in the hotel room. Yes, you do know it.

## they don't think I had a good motive

Yesterday they dared to say I was never married to David, much less divorced. They argued that if I ever did have his child, it must have been such a hushed-up business that not even Papa Woodward found out. I explained to them again and again that I gave my son to an adoption agency in Panama, using a false name which unfortunately I don't recall any longer. In that case, they pointed out, very little can be done to prove I am right. I even gave them the name and address of my parents there, but they don't appear to be very interested. I saw smiles and not very much conviction on their faces during the questioning. They still haven't called a lawyer for me, nor have they had me examined by a psychiatrist either, despite the fact that it is obvious that for them I really have gone out of my mind. They are only worried about my motive. I tell them what it was, and they don't believe me. Sometimes I thinking I am losing my mind. You know quite well, Carmen, that you returned to Panama after the divorce and had your child there. It looked so like him. Night after night, alone in your room at your parents' house in Las Tablas, you begged the Virgin that if it were a boy, please don't let it look like him. But he was the very picture. Your parents were very understanding. It was only to them that you told the truth. Neither they nor anyone else in Panama had known of David's existence before your return. But it wasn't because of what people would say that you took him there so they could look for adoptive parents for him. Probably you were selfish in your attitude, since it bothered you that the baby's every movement and every look reminded you of David so much that you transferred to him all the hatred you had stored up. But even though you were so selfish, that in itself was at bottom a kind of love, and love is always protective.

It was enough that you were pregnant when you arrived back in town for criticism and judgment to be raised. Your mistake was not what everyone thought. But you felt that not letting anyone know you had gotten married in the United States and then divorced again would soften the shame consuming you for having loved David so futilely. It was preferable for your own people to consider you a light woman. Even your childhood friends thought the worst. They said the gringos had corrupted you with their money and they called you a whore behind your back while to your face they pretended understanding smiles. Maybe you yourself would have thought the same about someone else. Nonetheless, when you realized you could not live in peace among your own folks, you asked your parents to pardon you for the trouble you had caused them, encouraged them to go to the capital if the rumors hurt them too much, and returned to Miami. As you had done before meeting David, you continued to attend classes at the university while working to pay for your studies.

Maybe all those experiences were not real, Carmen? Tell me if you can, you who still breathe in the empty corners of my mind, you who are not I and nevertheless are so much I, though no one believes me. Is it merely imagined, for example, the memory of that morning when David saw you eating breakfast in the coffee shop of the hotel where a couple of days before he had tried to kiss you in his room? The clear vision of him coming over to you in a determined way and asking if you cared if he sat at your table?

"I promise to behave," you remember him saying, but you didn't answer.

"I want to apologize for my behavior a couple of days ago, though I know there is no real excuse. I could blame it on the fact that I was drinking a little before. Or I could tell you that when I see a pretty girl I do things like that to see what kind of girl she is, since a lot of them just don't care. Both excuses would be true, but you don't have to believe either one of them. I'll just say that it's nice to find a decent girl from time to time, someone you can respect."

"I didn't know you were in your room or I would never have gone in," you said inattentively after listening to his speech.

"No, no, please," he exclaimed, patting your hand casually as it rested on the table. "I'm the one who is apologizing, remember?"

"You already did that."

"I won't ask you to pardon me because I see in your eyes—which are really very lovely—that you have already done so . . . And now I see it in that smile. Thanks a lot. I must go now. I've got some important business downtown."

"What part of the country are you from?"

"Wisconsin. I'll be staying here a couple of days longer. We probably won't ever meet again. My name is David Woodward."

"Mine is Carmen Robledo. I'm from Panama."

"Panama! I thought you would be Cuban or Puerto Rican. Is the Canal still ours?"

"It won't be much longer."

"Revolutionary?"

"Patriot."

"What does that mean? Maybe you can explain it to me with all the details before I leave for California Wednesday," he said, looking at his watch. "Tomorrow, for example. Would you accept an invitation to dinner?"

Was that conversation a dream? Tell me, Carmen. And the hours you spent dancing at Los Violines, and the nights that followed, with your visits to the best night clubs and finest restaurants, despite your inadequate dresses? The walks along the beach, the time you went in swimming naked, and afterward, stretched out on an old boat, his promises of love? And your fear of giving yourself to him knowing he had already extended his stay in Miami as long as possible and that he would leave the following day? And the way you felt when he came back three weeks later and you made love again? And your great happiness when he sent for you to get married? And what it meant at first to know that you were his wife and to keep the secret to yourself so that he would be more yours? Were those just dreams, Carmen, all those things that now seem so remote?

After the divorce you got checks from Papa Woodward on two occasions. Both times you tore them into pieces and sent them back without any explanation. Your father lost his job with the new change of government, and you had to swallow the humiliation of having to work as a waitress and maid in a hotel, which after all in the United States was not humiliating for the other students. There was a time when you were going to classes in the morning, tutoring several students in the afternoon (students in Spanish who paid you for it), and working at night as a waitress. When David reappeared you had just graduated with a degree in English from the University of Miami at Coral Gables, where you had come to live after returning from Panama. You know all this, Carmen, you have lived through it. Why don't they believe you, then?

\* \* \* \* \*

Scarcely had she opened her eyes when she encountered the glassy look of an absent blue firmness near the red pool which was spreading out and enveloping her. She screamed. She thought her son's eyes might acccuse her that way some day if he ever got to meet her. His facial expression kept looking for a way of going beyond its bounds, spreading terror to her face and freezing it there. She got up abruptly and ran into a corner of the hotel room, screaming. When someone slapped her hard enough on the face she understood that all the previous racket that she had hardly been aware of had been caused by the police breaking the door down.

I told them all the things that had happened to Carmen but what they really wanted to know was what had occurred that night, from the beginning. So it was that I told them about going for that drive down to the deserted beach. I tried to explain to them that Carmen had not just one but lots of motives to do what she did. I told them in detail the state of mind she was in during the dinner in David's hotel room afterward . . .

It had been a long while before they spoke in the luxurious room looking out on the beach. A waiter was setting the table carefully. David looked at her and she felt shrouded by those avid eyes while she turned her gaze aside toward the side window. When the waiter had gone he approached her and, taking her hands in his, invited her to sit down at the table. The meal was excellent, but she was not hungry. She only drank, somewhat compulsively, the sweet, heavy wine he was pouring for her. Through the wide open window there reached them the odor of the sea, brought in by soft breezes that made the curtains dance in an odd way. David never tired of making plans. Carmen was silent, pretending her interest was being awakened. The greater the effort he made to seem sincere, the more the sounds of those English words in that offensively melodramatic voice rubbed against her nerves. His remarks about different things were clumsy, to the point of making the blood churn through her temples, or perhaps it was the wine—or maybe it was everything together that was clouding her reason.

"By the way," said David coolly, putting a brusque note into the flow of conciliatory sentences that had preceded it, "was it a boy or a girl you had? I forgot to ask you. You never even wrote to tell me about it. I assume you put it up for adoption, or is it with your parents?"

"I never knew what it was," I lied. "It was already dead when they decided it was necessary to get it out of me."

"Oh! I didn't know," he murmured without raising his eyes from his plate. "Maybe it was better that way, don't you think? I mean, it would have been a great problem for you, being alone and taking classes and all." He took a swallow of wine. "But everything will turn out OK now, you'll see. We'll be more careful. You can start taking the pill again, but don't miss a single day this time . . ." He was talking to me as if he didn't recall the incident of a few hours back, or as if there were no danger at all of my getting pregnant. "I wouldn't want you to be so stupid as to ruin that marvelous body God gave you . . ." She thought he would add, "for my use and abuse," but it was merely his twisted expression trying to become a smile that took shape on that cheeky face now caught by the wine and the half-light. "But your body is terribly exciting, you know that, Carmen?" he whispered, trying to touch my breast from across the table. "I can't forget your cunt, it's so rich, so dark and fragrant, how it tastes . . . No other woman has it like you have, my love, I've told you that before, right?"

    I threw myself backward, nauseated. The blood was pounding in my temples. His hand came down on the edge of the table, curled over, almost twitching, like a spider. I felt dizzy.

    "Listen, why are you so nervous? It's just me, David . . . What's the matter? Why do you look at me like that? Are you crazy or something? Carmen . . . For God's sake . . . Drop that . . . No!"

    I had gotten to my feet with the knife for slicing the bread firmly in my hand. Bending over toward him I sank it in his breast, with all my might . . . once more . . . and again . . .

    "My God!" he stammered at the end of his surprise, but the blade no longer sought to enter him.

    It seemed useless for me to tell them that as I was collapsing, the only thing I could think of was the time I dreamed the telephone was ringing and when I answered it David's voice had been there begging me, "Give me another chance . . . another chance . . . another . . ." And as that echo was coming out of the receiver in spirals and screwing itself into my ear, I had managed to trap it there, twisting and twisting about frantically against my eardrum and trying to get out, pleading all the while, " . . . puhleeuhze . . . ," gradually losing its strength, and finally I was unable to hear its desperate reverberation, until the voice faltered completely and I sensed the face at the other end of the line changing from purplish to ashy-gray, and I vomited when I felt the surging of his blood had left my ears and was flowing swiftly into my mouth looking for a way out . . . That dream wouldn't have meant anything to the police, and that is why I kept it back.

But for my taste, David, your death was too quick. You should have suffered more, a lot more, as I began to conceive it that night after the outrage you committed. The long periods of pretended drowsiness that have been coming over me one after the other between fragments of events which they have managed to drag out of me have given me time to fantasize. And last night I had another dream which I did tell them today, but as if it had really happened that way after burying the knife in you that last time.

Noticing how you were leaning on the table holding yourself up in a grotesque way, with the knife buried to the hilt and your eyes popping out of their sockets with disbelief and fear both at once, suddenly I felt your own terror was invading me. You opened your mouth in an effort to scream, your hands were folding around the knife hilt, trying to pull it out. But then it seemed to hurt you all the more, and they seemed to be advancing across the table toward me, entreating me. I moved back. A blood stain was already dampening your white shirt when everything clouded over. It was the last thing I remembered, I told them, next to the vague sound of dishes breaking.

\* \* \* \* \*

"I love her and I will marry her no matter how stubborn you are. I can't go on being your puppet all my life, Father. This is the first decision that is really mine. I won't allow you to ruin it for me. Carmen is a good kid: sweet, good, intelligent, maybe a little shy, but I like that. I couldn't have slept with her without promising to get married. And after that I knew there was no reason I really had to marry her, but I liked the idea and I know that is because I love her."

That's part of what was in the letter they found in David's pocket. A police captain showed me a photocopy this morning. There was no date. This has managed to complicate things even more. The police are convinced now that the marriage mentioned in the letter as about to take place must really be our first one. More than ever now they doubt the fact that we were ever divorced and that a son of David's is living in Panama. I have told them this surely must have been an old letter, written years ago when David and I had begun to go out together, a letter that for some reason he never had sent, that perhaps for some reason he had decided to show me that night in the hotel. They don't believe me. And they can't do that for one very simple reason: Papa Woodward is alive. Or at least, that's what they tell me. I still haven't seen him.

\* \* \* \* \*

I don't like the lawyer they assigned me today. He gives me the impression he is more interested in proving their theories than in the true things I tell him. He says Papa Woodward has hired the best lawyers in order to get me convicted. If the old man is really alive, why would David lie to me? He seemed so happy now to be able to make his own decision . . . and now I've missed my period.

My God, how mixed up I am. My own memories are getting tangled in their versions. Can they be right? Could I have dreamed my marriage, the divorce? Can I have dreamed you, my son, so lonely and far away, without your mother? Why do I have then this sensation of reality trying to make its way out from between my legs, tumble around at my breasts, and suck out my soul? Why do you suffer, Carmen, if you really know now that what is troubling you is not the blood you saw when you came to?

\* \* \* \* \*

I'm tired of thinking. It frightens me being so alone. I don't believe they are sending my letters home. The other one, the one with those vivid memories, has gone. It was a slow process, but today I've demonstrated this fact because I've been unable to evoke her. Maybe she stayed in Panama with her son. I don't know how much time has gone by, how long it will be before something new happens.

I hardly sleep. And when I do manage, an obsessive, recurring dream takes possession of me: lots of babies are suckling at my firm, small breasts, and they are white and fat as pigs; they have the watery eyes of Papa Woodward, David's expression on all their faces, and dollar bills tickling me in place of their hands.

# the owl whose wings stopped beating

*For Rogelio Sinán*

When he inhaled this time he was too deeply shot through with the pain to resist the fathomless current of icy cold that was getting into his bones. His eyes collapsed shut while his body was coming to feel as though packed in a distant inertia like cotton balls. The silence was a dark, blinded owl disintegrating with a spasmodic fluttering of wings after its mask had been stripped away. Beneath the powerful overhead lamps was heard only the slight sound of surgical instruments going from hand to hand, utilized, returned, exchanged for others, used again, passing always through the silent hygiene of their rubber gloves.

"Heart?"
"Strong."

"Drill."

Multiple voices and distorted lights shouting and glittering. Filaments of voices constantly spinning cease to be voices and turn into brilliant colors, then into voices again, then colors that keep spinning in circles of voices turning into colors . . .

Armies of spots are vibrating, shouting, glittering in tanks filled with sensitive gray material. Dozens of macabre eyes appear, popping out of their sockets like flies being knocked off a strip of sticky flypaper. Blinking eyes meet and cross each other's paths in an infinite procession, a monstrous, intermittent zigzag. The eyes dissolve and their ashes keep falling into the void. Legions of worms born from the ashes before these reach the depths remain floating restlessly all squeezed together in the midst of infernal whispers, whispers, whispering . . .

A horrifying sound, piercing, resonant, even more piercing, is rattling the foundations of that shattered craneum from outside, another world . . . The worms flee in all directions.

Boring boring in he discovers fragmented memories . . . distant voices . . .

Large patio . . . rocks and tall grass . . . children playing . . . They are running, jumping . . .

"Look, Sr. Valdéz, Miguelito broke his arm . . . running on the patio . . . It seems one of his friends stuck out his foot, he fell over a rock . . . the weight of his body on his arm . . ."

"I'm afraid . . . ! Where is my mother? I'm afraid . . . "

"Shall we call her, sir?"

"Yes, that would be best."

"What happened to my arm? Why does it look this way? It's all twisted."

"Quiet down, Miguelito . . . We're going to call your mama."

"This is the second time . . . They just got through taking the cast off. First in Costa Rica, last year . . . They said if I broke it again they'd have to cut it off. I don't want them to cut off my arm! Don't let them cut it off! Please . . . don't let them . . . !"

A pair of glasses floats over the branch of a gigantic mango tree. Beneath, like an immense garden where birds are flying from cloud to cloud instead of butterflies from flower to flower, a blue sky spotted with flakes of foam in different shapes. Very high above, the ocean with huge waves forming whitecaps.

Thousands of fish fall suddenly from the ocean into the sky like enlarged drops of rain sheathed in a slippery elasticity. Below, the birds, all singing together, look up, open their beaks, and swallow the fish being rained down endlessly by the ocean. One fish lands on the glasses still floating above the branch, hurling them down.

In the earth that has replaced the sky with its beaks, representatives of countless varieties of birds are digging a hole. A sudden burst of screeching marks the beginning of a serious dispute. They recall that there should be four varieties of hummingbirds given the honor of interring the glasses, since these birds are so tiny. Out of two fish held together with a thorn they make a cross which they set up over the grave. Then they chant hymns that are difficult to interpret.

"I touched the optic nerve . . . !"

"Continue, doctor."

"This is too close . . ."

"We'll try to reduce the pressure afterward so that no distorted images remain. Take it out now, doctor . . ."

A nose is making its way through the park. In a little while it encounters a mouth. The mouth is moving its lips back and forth but the nose doesn't seem to understand. Then the nose makes its nostrils dilate and retract but it doesn't succeed in communicating with the mouth. It only manages to show through pantomime that it is capable of smelling. Both fragments continue their progress through the park. Almost immediately they are intercepted by a pair of ears. The mouth speaks to them, and they seem to understand but cannot answer back. All of them together start moving once more. On coming close to a bench the nose perceives a slight odor of salt. The mouth opens its lips and sticks out a tongue just in time to catch a tear falling from the eye that is resting on the bench. The ears listen when the mouth speaks to the eye. When the eye sees the mouth and its companions, it allows another tear to fall which is swallowed by the mouth before it reaches the ground.

"But then, Professor, Darwin's theory as you interpret it . . ."

"Science has advanced a good deal since Darwin . . . Some theories have been amplified, others discarded, some concepts are almost like laws today . . . There is no doubt that evolution . . ."

"What do we do with the Bible, then, Professor? Padre Damián

*the owl whose wings stopped beating* 169

says that . . ."

"I don't know anything about theology. There are those who try to reconcile . . ."

"If the business about Adam and Eve was symbolic, the divine inspiration that is attributed to the Old Testament . . ."

"My mother says that the blacks look like . . ."

"Your mother is a racist."

"A few days ago I read that someone was claiming a certain find as an explanation of the missing link. It seems that Africa is . . ."

A man approaches. He pulls another eye out of his shirt pocket and exclaims, "They were floating in a little lake near here. I think it was a lake of tears. Do they need one more for this get-together? "

When it sees the other one the eye jumps out of the man's hand and lands with a sharp sound on the bench. Both particles move to one side in a nervous greeting. The ears have heard the man's words and are leaping about with joy. The nose is quivering with the smell of a human being. The mouth, licking joyfully at the air with its tongue, says with feeling, "Now we're all together again!"

The man thinks about the lack of symmetry on the bench; he takes out paper and pencil, draws the outlines of a face, puts the paper down and arranges the two eyes, the nose, the two eyes, and the mouth over the face, filling up the empty space to suit his own taste. From his pants pocket he takes out a small mirror that he holds in the air over the face so the eyes can appreciate their new look.

"That's what they say around here, everyone is talking about it, how do I know . . . ?"

"Just gossip, woman, don't you know what people are like?"

"Look, Jaime, it's better to tell me the truth . . . Because if I ever find out that it's true that you . . ."

"You couldn't hurt a fly, don't make me laugh . . . Why, just to keep from stepping on some ants that time we went for a walk . . ."

When the eyes see themselves in the mirror, they jump out of their sockets and run terrified toward a spherical object the size of an ashtray lying on the grass behind the bench. The other parts have a feeling that the harmony has been broken anew and begin to move about in a nervous grin which turns into a vicious circle. They lack the sight to see the phenomenon they sense. The mouth whines disconsolately.

"I can't extract it without cutting through the nerve permanently."

"It is necessary to risk the eye, doctor. Proceed. Anesthetist, another quarter . . ."

The man watches the object rising in spirals until it is lost to sight. Scratching his head, he says, "I thought they would be happy to have the form of a human face. They didn't seem to be related the right way. Everything is so out of order today. It almost makes you think they aren't really human elements. Perhaps in some other dimension they may have another arrangement, another kind of symmetry. Or is it simply that the harmony of the parts is no longer valid?"

Seizing the nose, ears, and mouth from the bench (while the latter complained of being maltreated by the repressive forces that have the world in their grip), he throws them all to drown in the lake of tears, separated by the liquid distances that have been increasing as the water rolls down slopes that are pitched in opposite directions, opening up the lake like a huge silvered star above the green grass of that tranquil park.

The gas is beginning to come in through the byways of consciousness, filling empty spaces of time, awakening reminiscences of another, now forgotten smell . . . diabolical eyes watching me from over the mask of purity . . . pieces of cloth that other hands hold out to mop up the little drops . . . one falls on my cheek and they dry it off immediately . . . a far-off voice telling me, "Count as far as you can and soon you'll be asleep. You won't feel anything . . ." I make a conscious effort to count: "One, two, three, four, five, six, seven, eight, nine, ten, elev—" until I feel my tongue becoming very heavy. But every once in a while, as if from a great distance, I sensed the doctor's voice or my mother's, and I had to begin all over again . . . "He's very restless . . . hold his arm, nurse . . . it seems as though it's not having any effect on him . . . his nerves, doctor . . . give him more ether . . . my poor little boy . . .the second time this has happened. . . don't be afraid, Miguelito, your mommy is here . . . everything is going to be all right . . . try to relax, you are so tense . . . think of nice things so the doctor can fix your arm . . . there, that's it . . . rest now, your mommy's not going to leave you . . ." and the heavy mouth with lips and a fear stronger than the pain itself getting in through my spine, making me resist strange visions that are invading me with each new absorption . . . "Why are you laughing? Why are they laughing this way?" he shouted at them from the ground . . . "Make them stop, make them stop . . ." They were surrounding me as they lifted me up, and for a moment I think it is because of my glasses that had gotten broken on the sharp edge of the rock but then I see another sharp edge coming out of my lacerated flesh, and I remember what that doctor in Costa Rica said he would do to me if it ever happened again and—"Mommy, pretty Mommy, my arm!" he shouted. "My arm . . . it's my arm again . . ."

A zoo. And the animals? It's still early, they must be sleeping. But no, they're coming out now. They're men. Human beings in the zoo. No, it's not a "zoological" park. The sign says

## HOMOLOGICAL GARDENS

In one cage is a man of the Caucasian race. An Asiatic in another. An African black specimen over there. The signs hanging above each of the cages indentify them. And a little further on in cages side by side, the predecessors of *Homo sapiens*:

## JAVA MAN
## CRO-MAGNON MAN
## NEANDERTHAL MAN

Seated within their cages whose bars are set close together, they are all wearing glasses and munching on bananas while staring out toward unknown points. Along the pathways that go beside the cages the visitors are walking. An elephant and her little one, a tiger with three little tiger cubs, a single giraffe, a curious wolf, a porcupine with a scowl on its face, a sleepy lion . . . From the nearby forest come other animals in what seems to be a well organized outing in pursuit of knowledge.

Two monkeys of middling height come to a halt in an arrogant way in front of those they recognize as the first integral apes of the human race. They begin to laugh, splitting their sides. The Java man shakes the heavy bars back and forth in a sudden explosion of rage. The other two men emit grotesque sounds while they stomp furiously on the floor. The monkeys finally decipher the sounds and form words in their brains: "How and why am I like this?" and "Someone shit on the world." And laughing uncontrollably they withdraw, leaping.

A huge anthropoid ape jumps down from a tree and makes his way toward an open cage. He takes several steps rather erect on his hind legs, feeling his great size, proud of something. But suddenly he seems to get tired of the farce and continues his progress on all fours. Though less so than the other three encaged beings, he approximates humans in his bearing and musculature. Strong and extremely hairy, he has a long head and broad face with sunken, half-blind eyes that make him seem like an idiot compared with his neighbors who are wearing glasses. He enters the cage and shuts the door. After picking up a large wooden sign from the ground, he stretches his arms out through the bars and hangs it from a hook so that it can be read from outside:

MAN-MONKEY

It says this in big red letters. Below them, between parentheses and in white letters, it reads: *Missing Link*. The anthropoid sits down on the ground negligently without noticing the dark owl that has silently just come to rest on top of the cage and is now contemplating him while he masturbates happily until a rising explosion of sperm causes the bird to fly away, and then with a smile the man-monkey stretches out to rest.

"Did you get it all?"
"I think so."
"You can't just "think," doctor; that's the first thing you learn."
"Twenty-two calibre."
"Yes, that's all of it."
"That's not so bad. I'll relieve the pressure on his eye now."
"If he lives he'll be a vegetable."
"Please, nurse!"
"I'm sorry, doctor."
"Heart?"
"Very weak."
"Hurry.

Masks, masks, masks... they appear, disappear... Blue, green, red, yellow, colorless masks... Long, narrow, round, ugly, tiny, pretty masks detaching themselves and fading out . . . A sticky substance emerging from the slit between the lips . . . lips . . . Laughter turning into guffaws, becoming grimaces that turn into smiles and then into guffaws from grimaces from smiles quivering unrestrained. . . ha . . . ha . . . ha . . . ha . . . ha . . . ha . . . until they all fade away when the voices come in.

"To be accepted into our theatrical group you have to pass a test . . . test . . . test . . ."

"A test? What kind of test?"

"We must evaluate your histrionic abilities in the general areas of expression, diction, and memory . . . memory . . . memory . . ."

"Histrionic? And what must I do . . . do . . . do . . ."

"The first test consists in projecting the character of an owl . . . owl . . . owl . . ."

"An owl? how strange! Why an owl? I don't understand . . . stand . . . stand . . ."

"You have a peculiar likeness to that bird. Now, concentrate, think that you're an owl and act like one. Concentrate . . . Close your eyes . . . That's it . . . Now you're an owl and you are perched on a branch on a dark night . . . night . . . night . . ."

"I'm an owl . . . , yes, an owl . . ."

"Marvelous. Wonderful . . . ha . . . ha . . . ha . . . ha . . . ha . . . ha . . . See how he flaps his wings and moves his eyes so solemnly over you as if meditating the beauty of his humanness . . . ha . . . ha . . . ha . . ."

"And now what do I have to do? I'm not an owl any more."

"You are mistaken, you lovely ugly bird, you will always be an owl. The following test will also measure your concentration. As well as your reserves of energy. First I will take off my pants and throw myself on that old mattress face down. You will approach slowly and . . ."

"No, no, no . . . You're all just . . ."

"Not all of us, little owl, not all of us, but we do have our self-respect . . . Come on, now, I'm getting tired in this position with my butt in the air."

"No, no . . ."

Stony bursts of laughter rain down like rocks bouncing everywhere. They break open as they strike against the walls of the brain and new bursts of laughter come rolling out . . . ha . . . ha . . . ha . . .

ha . . . ha . . . ha . . . ha . . . And suddenly, total darkness, and the world is covered with quivering guffaws until it seems to be coming apart because it can hold them back no longer . . . But the echo of other voices freezes the laughter and takes its place . . .

"It doesn't really make any difference to her, as long as I give her what she wants when she wants it," remarks a tired-looking penis that is indolently lying back on a huge double bed.

"But the time will come when you're too worn out to make her happy," a pair of breasts exclaim in unison, whose rosy nipples appear beneath the pillow lying on the carpeted floor.

"Don't worry so much. It's not so bad," mutters the shriveled penis.

"If I can share you, she should, too, and let's be open about it; forget these stupid conventions and legaliities," babbles the irritated vagina lying at the foot of the bed.

"Well, yeah, of course," says the penis and goes to sleep.

From out of nowhere streams of thick blood are surging, invading the streets and sidewalks, pouring out through doors and windows, drowning everything that breathes, and finally settling down to form puddles that keep evaporating in the sunlight, ponds behind houses that no one visits now.

"You look like an owl with those glasses, Uncle Miguel!"

"I have to use them all the time now."

"Look at yourself in the mirror. Your face is like an awful owl!"

"Don't call me that, Pepe. I am a professor of biology, and your uncle, and you ought to show some respect for me."

"But it's true. You're an owl. Look at yourself!"

"Why doesn't anyone respect what I am? My God! It's true, I am an owl."

"Owly, owly, my uncle is an owly . . . No, don't take them off . . . See, without them you aren't an owl any more."

"Without them I can't see . . . And besides, whether I've got them on or not, who am I? I'm not sure now . . ."

The seconds are flying by in the operating room. Ten pairs of very open eyes are fixed on that opened head. Their foreheads are sweating. The masks stretched taut over their noses hardly move at all.

"His heart has stopped beating."

"Quick. We'll give him a shot of electricity."

The sequence of images has become paralyzed. Clinically, the patient has ceased to exist. Nevertheless, as in a moving picture that has come to a halt leaving an image frozen on the dimly illuminated screen, a hazy vision remains suspended in his mind. During that lapse—timeless within but laden out there with the suspense of the struggle in which the surgeons are joined—no one is conscious, on either of the two sides of reality, of that unique crystallized image which has shaped the torture of a memory:

*A man with the head of an owl lies naked on the also naked body of a woman with no head. Another woman with the face of a hyena is standing near the bed watching the scene, pistol in hand, eyes and mouth enormously exaggerated in the very pale face, the door to the room open behind her. The three figures are in positions that betray movements abruptly interrupted . . .*

"Slight beating . . . very slight."

"Stop the electric shock. I'll do a massage."

When the blood finally reaches the area of the brain, a silent flowing of images occurs . . .

*Hyena-face laughs unrestrainedly, her features skipping all about, as she shoots the head of the owl . . .*

"It's starting to normalize."

"Suture."

*Owl's head falls off, rolls to the floor, disintegrates . . .*

"It would be better if he were to die."

"What is important is to live, nurse."

"Like this?"

*In a widening red pool, the body of the man is shaking in spasms still sunk in the body of the woman with no head . . . slow spasms . . . unhurried . . . painful . . .*

"What is happening, doctor?"

*The chilling laughter of the hyena resounds with an echo that becomes progressively discordant as it fills the room and becomes space without time.*

## while typing

Though without even the slightest idea of how he would be able to wrap up the ending of this story as if in a glove, he sensed a slight vanishing of uncertainty in the air, something like the murmuring of ghostly presences in their final throes. He didn't know how to explain it. A strange tingling was making his hand tense up over the keyboard of the typewriter. Now the keys seemed to dissolve in a gray dance of letters.

Later, resting his gaze on the big clock occupying the center of the wall opposite, he became aware that the midnight chimes now being authenticated by those two very black arrows actually were coinciding with the first strokes which his memory brought him of another, more intangible midnight. In his head they kept peeling in time with the more immediate ones here in his room, but, because more intimate and personal, those others were resounding with a greater sense of reality.

After the final echoes had faded, everything became petrified in a delayed silence. The hazy scene in his brain that had been on the verge of springing out like some animal just freed from its cage disappeared completely, and the will to go on writing fell away from his tensed fingers. He looked at the papers beside him, fearing to understand what had burst from his mind in uncontrollable paroxysms during the previous few minutes. He read:

"I'm going to leave you," his wife had told him at the very moment of that New Year when, as the last page of the calendar was being consumed, it gave itself over now to the mathematical, cold time of the other one about to be born, bringing its gloomy perspectives along with it.

They had gotten dressed in their separate rooms; as a compromise they would attend the sumptuous ball the Club gave every year for its members. Now catching sight of her, his eyes quickly ran over that severely made-up mannequin's face; more and more it was showing the evident traces of a starlet being pushed by age. They went on to her round, deep neckline, as revealing as an open window through which the preambles to twin gratifications were beginning to appear. They descended past her waistline, with its renewed diminutiveness, and came to rest on the half of her white, bare thighs suddenly visible where the soft folds of her skirt abruptly ended.

"You think you're going out like that?"

"This is the way I'm going to leave you," she said; her gaze was a challenge as strong as her figure.

"Before or after the dance?"

"Preferably after. I want to have some fun for a little while."

"By using me to show yourself off first."

"Oh, they will envy you."

"If I left you alone for a minute you wouldn't even know who had you last."

"That's my affair."

"All right."

"At dawn I'll leave with somebody or other."

"Exactly."

"If I get bored, it might be sooner."

"Naturally."

"Unless I find someone who interests me the moment we get there."

"Don't think you're going to get me all riled up. What we had was never more than a farce."

"On my part?"

"The sooner we get there the sooner you can say when and where you'll go," he said, changing the subject. "Meanwhile, let me finish this."

She came over to him slowly. She had been looking down at her breasts almost without realizing it, as if finding it odd that he no longer let his eyes come to rest on them. He, on the other hand, went on calmly typing his story. They would go when she asked him.

"Don't you like it?" she whispered, standing close to him.

"You mean, all that perfume?"

"My dress."

"You look better naked."

"The others don't know that."

"Oh, really?"

His eyes had intentionally focussed on hers, made up as they had looked the night he first met her selling cheap cigarettes to evil-smelling customers, occasionally even to sailors.

"The ones at the Club don't know it."

"They will think it."

"And they'll want me all the more."

"Less."

"More."

"Less. I know."

"Don't you want to?"

"Want to what?"

"Want what's going to happen?"

"I might want something."

"Like what?"

"Like not going anywhere now, like doing something else. But not what you're thinking."

"Just so you won't have to get mad because of my dress, right?"

"Of course not."

"Well why, then?"

"It's better not to invite questions."

"What questions? And all those stares, too, of course."

"The questions," he insisted with a slight gesture of impatience.

"The ones they would ask me afterwards, alone," he added sharply.

"Are you talking about when I leave you, maybe?"

He stopped looking at her and his lips distended in a grimace. She had a smile on her face; her fingers were running slowly back and forth over the upper part of the chair's back, managing to avoid touching her husband's neck.

"I'm talking about when I leave you," he said, his face masked with a sudden cloak of serenity.

"You leave me? You leaving me?" she laughed unintentionally; this was a surprise to her. She well knew the weakness of this man who tonight was trying to pass himself off as indifferent. There had been five years of outward appearances thrown in the faces of friends, impresarios, and relatives in an effort to prevent rumors before they got started, but she knew the truth that was gnawing at his bones. "Look, we'd better go now. It's getting late."

"Yes, you're so right."

He stood up, suddenly very tired. His head was spinning. She went on smiling; her features began to dance about on her face that was so carefully covered with powder. Her perfume was getting into him through his eyes and his nose, making him dizzy.

"Let's go, then. What's the matter with you?"

*He wanted to explain to her that it would seem a little odd to arrive at the Ball on the arm of someone who was deceased. What would people think? He might endanger his position. How to justify such behavior? No, she would have to stay here ...*

He stopped reading. Right there was where the inspiration had been cut short. More than half a page of white space was left on the piece of paper before him. The chimes of the old clock had shattered an ending that was just beginning to be worked out.

The silence that was now lengthening by the walls suddenly disappeared through the half-opened window with the snap of a light being turned on in the back. Immmediately the new light fused with what was emerging from his own lamp over the desk. He assumed she must finally be ready for the dance.

As he was standing up the lost inspiration overcame him unexpectedly. His fingers began to run eagerly over the keys. He was panting. The words were taking shape in continuous, tireless streams. From some part of his consciousness the fear that his wife might speak and interrupt him clutched at his nerves. He couldn't let this new idea get away from him this time. He intensified the level of his concentration as the paper was filling up with letters.

Done. He was sweating. He pulled the paper out of the machine. With a premonition of the footsteps behind him, he read:

*The two shots were not heard outside. At that moment a multitude of deafening artificial fires, whistles, and sirens began vibrating. Through the window he saw glittering explosions of light opening out into vivid multicolored fans against the background so conveniently black.*

*He senses some hands that seem inexplicably cold coming to rest on his shoulders. He would have had to stop breathing entirely in order not to inhale that perfume. He turns slowly. She has put on that damned dress with the deep neckline after all. In that case, what are his decisions for, around this house?*

# shame

"The New Panama School, please."

The man put the car in gear and she made herself comfortable in the back seat.

You could see buildings under construction wherever you looked. It was a splendid day, the heat was overwhelming, but the woman amused herself watching people, cars, houses go past, as if they were leaping into view and quickly falling behind instead of herself being carried ahead by the rapid movement of the taxi transporting her.

It was the first time she had visited Panama. Her husband happened to have been invited by the city's Chamber of Commerce to give a series of lectures on economic matters. They had only come for five days, but she would convince him to stay the entire week. We'll be able to visit interesting places, get to know the people, go to the beach. They had just arrived the night before, and they still had had no contact with Panamanians, except for the people in the hotel.

Now she is making her way to the place where, according to the local newspapers, a national folklore festival will take place. Michael's talks bored her enormously. The truth is that she doesn't understand anything about business, nor does it interest her. Sometimes she wished that her husband would neglect his company office a little, busy himself with me more, with my tastes. Cultural things are important, too. It would be fun to watch those famous national dances performed in their *empolladeras*, a kind of local native dress, to become familiar with that typical clothing usually seen only in photographs, and to see those other dances called *cumbías* and *tamboritos* that her Panamanian friends studying languages at the University of Colorado used to talk about so.

"Is it very far, señor?" she asked the chauffeur when she realized they had already spent about half an hour driving.

"It's a long way, señorita; in the outskirts. We took a long time getting out of the city. Because of the traffic. About fifteen minutes more, now."

"Señora. But thank you."

"Since you're so young it never occured to me you might be married. You're not from around here, right? You have a slight foreign accent."

"No, I just arrived."

She knew right away she shouldn't have said that.

"Alone?"

She saw his eyes scrutinizing her in the rear vision mirror. She would have to be careful with this fellow.

"With my husband."

"From the U.S.?"

"Please don't be such a busybody."

"Busybody? But it was only an innocent question—señora."

They were going faster now. Too fast. Oh, I hope we get there soon. She kept encountering those mocking eyes in the mirror. They seem to be stuck there, looking at me. Instinctively she sought to button up her blouse, but she already had it properly closed, despite the heat. And that man was still looking at her. Sometimes I don't wear anything down below, but I just happened to today. The man was not watching the road. He could be dangerous. In several senses. I don't see any houses alongside the highway now. The cars going in the opposite direction are beginning to get scarcer.

There was a moment when the man managed to turn his head around to look at her. She tightened her thighs, straightened out the pleats in her skirt. She didn't understand why there briefly came to her the image of her husband making love with her in the back of a car that time shortly before their wedding. More than fifteen minutes had gone by and they still hadn't arrived. She imagined the serious faces of the bankers and all their managers listening to Michael in some open hall. They probably hadn't brought their wives with them. The eyes still examining her. As if from the beginning of time, and until the end of time. Ever since I was fourteen my girl friends used to envy me the quality of my breasts, their texture, their firmness. And later on there had been that boy who looked Mexican or like an Arab. A chill went down her spine, making her change her position. The air seemed more humid.

"We should have arrived by now, shouldn't we?"

No reply. She pressed close to the door. She looked for the door handle in the darkness that she only just now had begun to notice. Outside, you could see a few lights off to the right, far off. There wasn't any handle. Or else she didn't find it. Her hands were sweating. She wanted to protest, tell him to go back, or perhaps to leave her here. The words wouldn't come. The car stopped sharply.

"Get out." He was dark, average height, a little bald. He was pointing to the path. I'll have to break into a run whenever I can. She got ready to do so. Once when she had left a masked ball with her boy friend two guys had followed them. I don't want to remember, I don't want to. They had beat him up, but she ran, ran, ran, just as it would be a good thing to be doing now. Space itself put up some resistance before her, as if the air were made of thick waves interposing themselves in front of her body. Still she intended to start running when they got to a clearing some way off from the highway. She felt hands on her shoulders, making her turn around. What could have happened to her boy friend? They've nearly caught up with me, I hope they don't hurt me. Her eyes were burning, she didn't want to open them. Just fifteen years old, and now the tallest one is getting on top of me. She screamed when she saw that other body being shown her, it was so hairy, so naked. Michael is circumcized. She shut her eyes. She hears a snap. Terrified, she opens them again and finds herself in the consulting room.

"You're all right now. You can rest. Take this, it's only a cool drink."

She must have looked him in confusion, urging an explanation out of him, because right away she heard the doctor saying, "You killed him in self defense. Everyone will have to believe you, even your husband."

The confusion continued. She began to recognize the voice when she was able to associate the meaning of words with their significance.

"The taxi driver attacked you, and you simply reacted in self-defense. It's not a serious thing. You must calm yourself down now, señora."

"If you say so I believe it. But the truth is I don't recall what happened before that, those moments before."

"It could be dangerous now to force your memory. You forgot the details themselves because you are afraid."

"What is it I'm afraid of, doctor?"

"That the past will be repeated, perhaps with your consent, perhaps not."

"I don't understand."

He smiled. The woman hands the half-full glass to him and tries to sit up. Putting both his hands on her shoulders the doctor forces her to remain horizontal.

"You don't need to recall everything right now. The amnesia will start disappearing little by little, perhaps completely in a few days, when you are able to accept the situation as it happened. Maybe even during the hearing before the judge. But in the trial that I do not doubt will follow and that I expect will be quite brief, I'll hypnotize you again. There we should be able to go back to the moment when you were attacked, up until the moment when you hit that man with the rock."

"That last is the only thing I remember."

"It was the first thing you told me when you came in here this morning."

"I hit him once, and then again and again in a rage, without stopping. Until I got tired and saw him on the ground bleeding."

The woman, who was getting very stimulated, sat up on the

divan and with her closed fist was striking at the arm of the doctor's chair. He held her by the wrists and made her lie down again.

"Enough, enough—calm yourself now or I'll have to inject you with a sedative. Don't think about it any more, at least not now. You told me your husband doesn't know anything . . ."

"No, nothing. I got back quite late last night, and I couldn't tell him. We have to leave in less than a week. A trial would complicate everything horribly, it might keep us here for a long time."

"What are you trying to tell me?"

"It will very likely be several days before they find the body, doctor. That was a very remote place. I drove myself back to the hotel in the taxi and left it several blocks away, with a flat tire so that it would look like an ordinary abandoned car . . . Listen, I only came to see you because I needed help. This morning I thought I would go crazy. I looked in the telephone directory and chose the first psychologist I came across. Keep my secret, and I'll pay you well. For the time we still have left in Panama you can give me some treatment to help me accept the situation or else to forget it, I don't know which is best."

"Do you realize what you are asking me? You have killed a man. That is the truth; it's not important that you did it in self-defense. But even if it were not exactly like that, with my assistance and that of a good lawyer, you would be cleared of wrongdoing. I'll get in touch with your embassy. I am certain they will help you to find one, it's their responsibility. I'll come to an agreement with him, and that way the defensive nature of your action will be quite clear. But you must help me. If you do so, I am certain we'll win the case."

"How will I explain it to my husband?"

"I'll talk to him first. He, and the police as well, will understand that you have suffered a very strong emotional shock, reason enough why you didn't immediately reveal what had occurred. Besides, you were suffering from amnesia which up till now has scarcely begun to abate."

"No, my husband wouldn't believe me."

"What is it that he is not going to believe?"

"It's a long story, doctor. When I was fifteen—"

"I already know about that story, or at least the important parts of it. It came out, though in pieces, when I hypnotized you. I assume your husband could question . . . But no, you surely have complete trust in each other."

"Things have not been very good between us lately. Perhaps because it keeps bothering him that he was not the first. Michael will not pardon me the least slip. He is so jealous that, when he thinks about previous "adventures" of mine that he found out about from certain indiscreet friends, he could easily imagine me involved in another one."

"No matter how distrustful he is, I don't believe he can really think that you would willingly get yourself entangled with a taxi driver in Panama the first day you were alone in this country."

"Michael is a lot like the Latin American macho in his attitude toward women. Before my first pregnancy obliged us to get married, he let me do anything. Now he would keep me locked up all day long if he could."

"Coming back to the point, I can assure you that your embassy is very influential in this country. I happen to know the consul, we've been friends for several years. If I speak to him, things will be done quietly, especially if, as you told me when you came in, your husband is an important businessman. One would have to put out a few thousand dollars, of course, but I don't think that would be a problem, would it?"

"In order to avoid a scandal, Michael is capable of almost anything. But frankly, doctor, I doubt very much that the people in the embassy would lend themselves to dishonest activities. I don't know how it would be in Panama, but in my country there are certain principles . . ."

"Look here, señora, let's get to the point and decide something soon. If you wish, I'll go right now to see the consul in order to explain the affair to the police and try to reach a solution as soon as possible. The essential thing is to keep it out from under the noses of the reporters, for the press blows everything out of proportion; they can distort things terribly, give them a sensationalist interpretation. And that is where, to tell you the truth, the embassy can exert pressure. Now if you have any other solution . . ."

"Doctor, it could be that that man was working for some business firm. I don't know about here, but at home the workers are usually unionized, which complicates things. Besides, he must have relatives or friends who would not keep quiet when they found out how he died.

It seems strange to me that you think it all so easy."

"I know my people, señora . . . But all right, if you don't wish to . . ."

"I'll give you two thousand dollars to forget the whole affair, aside from what you charge me for treatments the rest of the week."

"All right. But it will have to be two thousand five hundred in order to keep anyone else from getting involved."

"I'll bring you the money tomorrow. But you must give me your word that—"

"To talk about this with anyone in a way different from the way we have done would only bring on some serious risks which I would be unnecessarily involved in. You have my word. My amnesia will be complete, unlike yours."

"I know I have already taken up a lot of your time, doctor, but now that I am here, will you help me recall once and for all the details of the time I was attacked. I need to know."

"You and I both know, at this stage, that your insistence is clearly betraying what you suspect about yourself, though you may not recall all the details clearly, because you know yourself quite well. You were fortunate in coming to me, no matter how pedantic it may seem for me to say so. I am going to oblige you, but I should warn you that living through something like this again so soon is capable of producing a violent sense of guilt afterward, in case your suspicions are confirmed."

"That's a risk I must run. Above all because there are only a few scratches on my body, far too few, judging by the violence with which I was hitting him when I finally became conscious of what I was doing. Hypnotize me, doctor. Make me recall everything right up the end. I need to know if I was really defending myself or if it was out of shame more than anything that I killed him."

"Very well. But first I have to know if you have been promiscuous since being married."

"I've had lovers, if that's what you're referring to."

"That is what I'm referring to, señora. Oh, of course: what did you say your given name was?"

She told him, for the first time, without finding it too strange in the face of the sudden confidence with the doctor was treating her. Then she lay back on the divan once more and waited for the voice to guide her again through her mind during the moments lived since she had gotten into the taxi the previous afternoon.

It was a simple task now, oddly stimulating for both of them, despite the woman's inevitable anguish. The doctor went along proposing suggestions, introducing appropriate nuances into the events as they were taking place all over again. On getting to the scene when the taxi driver puts his hand on her shoulders, forcing her to turn around, the woman feels them pressing down on her now with a force which inexplicably does not correspond to the circumstances she is reliving. She hears someone asking her to open her eyes.

"Look at me," the voice orders. "This is what you like, Gisela. A naked man with an erection, any man . . . That's what you have always liked. You yourself are going to surrender to me, aren't you, dear?"

"Yes."

"As happened with the taxi driver."

"I didn't want to."

"But at the end you did want to."

"Yes!"

"And now, too."

"Yes, yes . . ."

The snapping sounds occurring so feebly minutes later scarcely manage to bring her mind back to the consulting room. In horror she returns in time to be aware of the doctor's hand as it halts in midair and descends awkwardly toward that body stabbed so many times because of this tardy eruption of shame. Gisela drops the scalpel, heaves aside the bulk covering her, and screams wildly without knowing any longer where she is.

*When New Flowers Bloomed: Short Stories by Women Writers from Costa Rica and Panama*, Enrique Jaramillo Levi, ed. Published by Latin American Literary Review Press.